When You Got A Good Thing

A MISFIT INN NOVEL
KAIT NOLAN

When You Got A Good Thing

Written and published by Kait Nolan

Copyright 2017 Kait Nolan

Cover design by Kait Nolan

All rights reserved, including the right to reproduce this book, or portions thereof, in any form.

AUTHOR'S NOTE: The following is a work of fiction. All people, places, and events are purely products of the author's imagination. Any resemblance to actual people, places, or events is entirely coincidental.

For the misfits. The family you make is the most important.

CHAPTER 1

"WELCOME TO O'LEARY'S PUB. What can I get you?" The greeting rolled off Kennedy Reynolds' tongue as she continued to work the taps with deft hands.

The man on the other side of the long, polished bar gaped at her. "You're American."

Kennedy topped off the pint of Harp and slid it expertly into a patron's waiting hand. "So are you." She injected the lilt of Ireland into her voice instead of the faint twang of East Tennessee. "You'd be expectin' somethin' more along these lines, I'd wager. So what'll it be for a strapping Yank like yourself?"

The guy only blinked at her.

So she wasn't exactly typical of County Kerry, Ireland. Her sisters would be the first to say she wasn't exactly typical of anyone, anywhere. It didn't bother her. But there was a line stacking up behind this slack-jawed idiot, and she had work to do.

"Can I suggest a pint of Guinness? Or perhaps you'd prefer whiskey to warm you through? The night's still got a bit of a chill."

He seemed to shake himself. "Uh, Jameson."

She poured his drink, already looking past him to take the next order, when he spoke again.

"How's a girl from—is that Texas I hear in there?—wind up working in a pub in Ireland?"

This again? Really? Kennedy repressed the eye roll, determined to be polite and professional

A big, long-fingered hand slapped the guy on the shoulder hard enough to almost slosh the whiskey. "Well now, I suppose herself walked right in and answered the help wanted sign." The speaker shifted twinkling blue eyes to Kennedy's. "That was how it happened in Dublin, now wasn't it, darlin'?"

"And Galway," she added, shooting a grin in Flynn's direction. "I'd heard rumor you were playing tonight. Usual?"

"If you'd be so kind. It's good to see you, *deifiúr beag*." His voice was low and rich with affection, the kind of tone for greeting an old lover—which was laughable. Flynn Bohannon was about as far from her lover as he could get. But it did the trick.

With some relief, Kennedy saw the American wander away. "Thanks for that."

"All in a day's work," Flynn replied.

"I've missed your pretty face." She glanced at the nearly black beard now covering his cheeks as she began to pull his pint of Murphy's Irish Stout. "Even if you are hiding it these days."

He grinned, laying a hand over his heart. "Self preservation, love."

"You keep telling yourself that." Kennedy glanced at the line snaking back through the pub. "I'm slammed here, and you're starting your set shortly. Catch up later?"

Flynn lifted the beer and toasted her before making his way toward the tiny stage shoehorned beside the fireplace, where the other two members of his trio were waiting.

Mhairi, one of the waitstaff, wandered over, setting her tray on the bar as she all but drooled in his direction. "Well now, I'd not be kickin' that one out of bed for eating crisps."

"Wait 'til you hear him play."

Mhairi glanced back at Kennedy, lifting a brow in question. "Are you and he...?"

"No. Just friends. The way there is clear, so far as I know."

The waitress smiled. "Brilliant." She reeled off orders and it was back to the job at hand.

As Kennedy continued to pour drinks, Flynn and his band tuned instruments. They weren't the same pair who'd been with him in Dublin, whom she'd traveled with for several weeks as an extra voice. That wasn't much of a surprise. It'd been—what?—a year or so since they'd parted in Scotland. Flynn would, she knew, go where the music took him. And that sometimes meant changing up his companions. He was as much an unfettered gypsy as she was, which was why they'd become such fast friends. But whereas he didn't mind a different city or village every night, she preferred to take a more leisurely pace, picking up seasonal work and staying put for two or three months at a stretch. Really immersing herself in the culture of a place. The ability to pause and soak in each new environment gave her both the thrill of the new and kept her from feeling that incessant, terrified rush of not being able to fit in everything she wanted to see or do. It was important to her to avoid that, to take the time to be still in a place and find out what it really had to teach her.

The itinerant lifestyle worked for her. She'd seen huge chunks of the world over the past decade, made friends of every stripe, picked up bits and pieces of more than a dozen languages. Many people saw her life as unstable. She preferred to think of it as an endless adventure. What did their stability give them? Consistent money in the bank, yes. But also boredom and stress and a suffocating sameness. No, thank you. Kennedy would take her unique experiences any day. Never mind that the desk jobs and business suits had never even been a possibility for her. She'd been ill-suited for the education that led to those anyway.

Across the pub, Flynn drew his bow across his fiddle and launched into a lively jig. The crowd immediately shifted its focus. Those who knew the tune began to clap or stomp in time, and a handful of patrons leapt up and into the dance. Kennedy loved the spontaneity of it, the unreserved joy and fun. As jig rolled into reel and reel into hornpipe, she found herself in her own kind of dance as she moved behind the bar. Flynn switched instruments with the ease of shaking hands, playing or lifting his voice as the tune dictated. He even dragged Kennedy in for a couple of duets that made her nostalgic for their touring days. His music made the night pass quickly, so she didn't feel the ache in her feet until she'd shut the door behind the last patron.

Flynn kicked back against the bar. "A good night, I'd say."

"A very good night," Kennedy agreed.

"Help you clean up?"

"I wouldn't say no."

They went through the motions with the other staff, clearing tables, wiping down, sweeping up. Mhairi went on home—disappointed. And Kennedy promised Seamus, the pub's owner, that she'd lock up on her way out. Then, at long last, she settled in beside the remains of the fire with her own pint.

Flynn lifted his. "To unexpected encounters with old friends."

"Why unexpected?"

"You said yourself you rarely stay more than three months in a place. You've already been from one coast of Ireland to the other. I didn't expect you back."

"I always seem pulled back here," she admitted. "The people. The culture. As a whole, I suppose Ireland has been as close as I've had to a home base over the past ten years. I've spent more collective time in this country than anywhere else combined since I started traveling."

"How long have you been in Kerry?"

"Coming up on three months."

"Thinking of settling?" he asked.

Was she? No. She still felt that vague itch between her shoulder blades that she got every time she'd been long enough in a place. She knew she'd be moving on soon, searching for the next place to quiet the yearning she refused to acknowledge. "Not exactly. I haven't decided where I want to go next. Which isn't the same thing." She took a breath and spilled out the news she'd told no one. "I've been contacted by a book editor in New York. She wants me to turn my blog into a book."

"Really?" Flynn's grin spread wide and sparkling as the River Liffey. "That's grand!"

It was the most exciting thing to ever happen to her, and she was glad to finally get a chance to share it. "I haven't said yes."

"Why not? Are the terms not to your liking?"

"We haven't gotten that far. I'm still thinking about it." Still looking for reasons to talk herself out of it.

"What's there to think about?" Flynn prodded.

"A book means deadlines and criticism and working on other people's schedules. None of those are exactly my strong suit."

"Bollocks. Every job you've had has been on someone else's schedule. As to deadlines, how hard can it be to take what you've already written and turn it into a book? *Not All Who Wander* is well-written, engaging, and personal. You're a talented writer."

On her better days, Kennedy could admit that. But it was one thing having her little travel blog, with its admittedly solid online following, be read and commented on via the anonymity of the internet. It was a whole other animal turning that into a book that lots of people could read. Or not read, as the case might be. That was opening herself up to a level of failure she didn't even want to contemplate.

"She's offered to fly me to New York to meet with her, and I'm thinking about taking her up on the offer. I might feel better about the idea of the project if we talk about it in person."

"And if you go back across the pond, will you finally take a detour home?"

At the mention of Eden's Ridge, Kennedy felt some of her pleasure in the evening dim. "It hasn't really been on my radar as an option."

"Maybe it should be."

She lifted a brow. "This from the man who's been on the go nearly as long as I have?"

"I travel and often, yes, but I've been home. I've seen my family. You've been running."

"I'm not running," she insisted.

"All right, not running. Searching, then. For something. In all your travels, have you found it?"

"How can I even answer that? I don't know what I'm looking for." But that was a lie. She knew what she was looking for and knew she wouldn't find it in any new country, on any new adventure.

"I'd say that's an answer in and of itself."

Kennedy scowled into her beer. "I've had my reasons for staying away from home."

"They aren't family. You've seen them since you left. So who?"

Her gaze shot to his.

Flynn jerked his shoulders and gave an easy smile. "Deduction, *deifiúr beag*. Who was he?"

Someone better off without me.

She was saved from answering by the ringing of her mobile phone. "Late for a call." Fishing it out of her pocket, she saw her mother's number flash across the screen. "Not so late back in Tennessee." She hit answer. "Hey, Mom."

"Kennedy."

At the sound of her name, she felt her stomach clench into knots. Because it wasn't her mother, and the strain in her eldest sister's voice was palpable. "Pru?"

"Are you sitting down?"

Absolutely nothing good could follow those words. "What?"

Beside her, Flynn straightened, setting his pint to the side.

"You're not on the street where you can accidentally walk into traffic or something are you?"

"I'm sitting. What the hell is going on? Where's Mom?"

Her sister took a shaky breath. "Kennedy, Mom was in an accident. Her car was in the shop, and she was in a loaner. We've had a cold snap."

"What?" Kennedy whispered.

"She…" Pru gave a hiccuping sort of sob. "She didn't make it."

The earth fell out from beneath Kennedy's chair, and she curled her hand tighter around the phone, as if that pitiful anchor would help. She didn't even recognize her own voice as she asked, "Mom's dead?"

She wasn't aware of Flynn moving, but suddenly he was there, his strong hand curling around hers.

"The doctors said it was all but instant. She didn't suffer. I… we need to make arrangements."

"Arrangements." She needed to get the hell off the phone. She needed to move, to throw something, to rail at the Universe because this…this shouldn't be happening. "I have to go."

"Kennedy, I know this is hard but—"

"I'm coming home. I'll be there absolutely as soon as I can. Call you back as soon as I know when." She hung up before Pru could answer.

"Do you want me to come with you?" Flynn asked.

He would. He'd cancel whatever bookings he had and fly across an ocean with her to face the grief and demons that waited in Eden's Ridge. But this was for her to do.

"No. I… No." Lifting her eyes to his, she felt the weight of grief land on her chest like a boulder. She'd never again hear her mother's laugh. Never smell her mother's favorite perfume. Never get a chance to tell her the truth about why she'd walked away. "Flynn."

Without word, without question, he tugged her into his arms, holding tight as the first wave crashed over her, and she fell apart, the phantom scent of violets on the air.

∼

CHIEF DEPUTY XANDER KINCAID parked his cruiser in front of the rambling Victorian that had been Joan Reynolds' home. He retrieved the covered dish of chicken enchiladas sent by his mama—the first wave of death casseroles that would soon fill the old kitchen to bursting—and headed for the front door. Despite its size, with its muted gray paint, the house tended to blend into the woods and mountains around it. Joan had loved this house. She'd always said it was a peaceful spot, a good place to heal and a good place to love. And she'd done exactly that for nearly twenty-five of her sixty-two years, filling the over-sized house with foster children who'd needed a home and someone to love them.

No telling whose home it would become now. Pru had moved back in. As the only one of Joan's adopted girls who hadn't moved away, she'd immediately stepped in to take over guardianship of Ari Rosas, Joan's most recent—well, her last foster child. But he didn't imagine Pru could afford the upkeep of the place on her income as a massage therapist—especially after the death taxes and probate lawyer had their way with the place. And what, he wondered, would happen with Ari, whose adoption hadn't yet been finalized?

Juggling the casserole dish, he rang the bell and waited. And waited.

Backing up on the porch, he craned his head to peer around toward the barn. Pru's car was there. He tried the knob and found it unlocked. Making a mental note to have a word with her about security, even here on the Ridge, he stuck his head inside. "Pru?"

She appeared at the head of the stairs, her big brown eyes red-rimmed from crying. "Sorry. I was just…" She tailed off, waving a vague hand down the hall.

"It's fine." He lifted the enchiladas. "Mama wanted me to bring these by. She thought with your sisters coming in, the last thing you or any of them would want to do is cook."

Xander watched as manners kicked in. Her posture straightened, her expression smoothing out as she locked down the grief.

"That's so kind of her." She came down the stairs and reached for the dish. "I'll just go put this in the kitchen."

He followed her back.

"No one's here just yet," she said, a false bright note in her voice, as if everything was fine and her world wasn't falling apart.

Xander waited until she slid the casserole into the fridge before he simply wrapped his arms around her. "Pru. I'm so sorry."

For a long moment, she stood there like a wooden post. Then a shudder rippled through her as her control fractured. Her arms lifted and she burrowed in.

"This shouldn't have happened," she whispered. "If she'd been in her own car instead of that tin can loaner, it wouldn't have."

Xander wasn't sure Joan's SUV would've handled the patch of black ice any better, but he remained silent. The fact was, nobody expected black ice in east Tennessee in March. Not when daytime temperatures were almost to the sixties. Joan's hadn't been the only accident this week. But she'd been the only fatality.

He ran a hand down Pru's silky, dark brown hair, hoping to soothe, at least a little. But this wasn't like middle school, when he'd been able to pound Derek Pedretti into the ground for making Pru cry by calling her fat. There was no one he could take to task, no one to be punished. Grief simply had to be endured.

"There are all these arrangements to be made," she hiccupped.

And no one here to help her do them, with Maggie off in Los

Angeles and Athena running her restaurant in Chicago. Xander deliberately avoided thinking about the final Reynolds sister, though he was sure that this would bring even her home. The idea of that caused his gut to tighten with a mix of old fury and guilt.

"What can I do to help?"

"Let me make you some coffee."

"Pru—"

"No really," she sniffed, pulling away. "I'm better when I'm doing something."

Xander didn't want coffee, but if she needed to keep her hands busy, he'd drink some. "Coffee'd be great."

She began puttering around the kitchen, pulling beans out of the freezer and scooping them into the grinder. Joan had loved her gourmet beans. It'd been one of the few luxuries she'd always allowed herself. As she went through the motions, Pru seemed to regain her control.

"Maggie's taking the red eye from LA, and Athena's flying out as soon as she closes down the restaurant tonight."

"Do either of them need to be picked up from the airport?"

"They're meeting in Nashville and driving up together in the morning, so they'll be here to help me finish planning the service. It's supposed to be on Thursday."

Xander didn't ask about Kennedy. Both because he didn't want to care whether she showed up, and if she wasn't coming, he didn't want to rub it in.

Pru set a steaming mug in front of him, adding the dollop of half and half he liked and giving it a stir. "Kennedy gets in day after tomorrow. There was some kind of issue getting a direct flight, so she's having to criss-cross Europe before she even makes it Stateside again. She's coming home, Xander."

He wasn't sure if that was supposed to be an announcement or a warning, but it cracked open the scab over a very old wound that had never quite healed.

She laid a hand over his. "Are you okay?"

This woman had just lost her mother, and she was worried about whether he'd be okay with the fact that his high school girlfriend, whom he hadn't seen in a decade, was coming home.

"Why wouldn't I be?"

Pru leveled those deep, dark eyes on his. "I know there are unresolved issues between you."

God, if only she knew the truth—that he was the reason Kennedy had left—she wouldn't be so quick to offer sympathy.

"It was a long time ago, Pru. There's nothing to resolve." Kennedy had made her position clear without saying a word to him. At the memory, temper stirred, belying his words. There were things he needed to say to her, questions he wanted answered. But whatever her faults, Kennedy had just lost her mother, too, and Xander wasn't the kind of asshole who'd attack her and demand them while she was reeling from that. Chances were, she'd be gone before he had an opportunity to say a thing. He'd gotten used to living with disappointment on that front.

He laid a hand over Pru's. "Don't worry about me. How's Ari?"

She straightened. "Devastated. Terrified. And…" Pru sighed. "Not speaking."

"Not speaking?"

"Not since I told her. She'd come so far living here with Mom, and this is an enormous setback. No surprise. Especially having just lost her grandmother last year." Pru continued to bustle around the kitchen, pouring herself a cup of coffee and coming to sit with him at the table. Her long, capable fingers wrapped around the mug.

"She upstairs?"

"Yeah. I was trying to get her to eat something when you got here."

"Poor kid. Have you talked to the social worker yet?"

"Briefly. Mae wants to let us get through the funeral and all the stuff after before we all figure out what to do."

"Who would've been named her emergency guardian if the adoption had gone through?" Xander asked.

"The four of us, probably. I know it's what Mom would've wanted. But there are legal ramifications to the situation, and the fact is, I'm the only one still here." She sighed. "We'll have to talk about it after. The one thing I know we'll all be in agreement on is that we want what's best for Ari."

"All four of you have been in her shoes, and you turned into amazing women. I know you'll do the right thing." Whatever that turned out to be.

Xander polished off the coffee. "I'm on shift, so I need to be getting back. But, please, if you need *anything*, Pru, don't hesitate to call. I'm just down the road."

She rose as he did and laid a hand on his cheek. "You're a good stand-in brother, Xander. Mom always loved that about you."

He felt another prick of guilt, knowing his own involvement with this family had been heavily motivated by trying to make up for Kennedy's absence. "Yeah well, I ran as tame here as the rest of you when we were kids. Especially when Porter was around." Giving her another squeeze, he asked, "Can I do that for you? Notify the rest of her fosters? I know you've covered your sisters, but there were a lot of kids who went through here over the years. I'm sure they'd like to pay their respects."

Her face relaxed a fraction. "That would be amazing. I'm sure we'll have a houseful after the funeral, but I need a chance to gird my loins for the influx. Mom kept a list. I'll get it for you."

As she disappeared upstairs, he wandered into the living room. Little had changed over the years. The big, cushy sofas had rotated a time or two. And there'd been at least three rugs that he could remember. But photos of Joan and her charges were scattered everywhere. Xander eased along the wall, scanning faces. A lot of them he knew. A lot of them, he didn't.

A shot at the end caught his attention. The girl's face was turned away from the camera, looking out over the misty mountains. She was on the cusp of womanhood, her long, tanned legs crossed on the swing that still hung from the porch outside, a book forgotten in her lap. Her golden hair was caught in a loose tail at her nape. Xander's fingers itched with the memory of the silky strands flowing through his fingers. She'd been sixteen, gorgeous, and the center of his world. The sight of her still gave him a punch in the gut.

"Here it is."

At the sound of Pru's voice, Xander turned away from Kennedy's picture. *Over and done.*

He strode over and took the pages she'd printed. "I'll take care of it," he promised.

"Thank you, Xander. This means a lot."

"Anytime." With one last, affectionate tug on her hair, he stepped outside, away from memories and the looming specter of what might have been.

CHAPTER 2

*B*Y THE TIME THE Uber dropped her off at the house —and she was deliberately *not* thinking about how much that ride from the airport actually cost her—Kennedy was so far past exhausted, she felt practically out of body. She hadn't felt right bothering her sisters for a ride, and she was used to finding her own way from one point to another. When one of her flights was canceled and another delayed for weather, it had taken a series of planes, trains, and automobiles to get her from the west coast of Ireland back Stateside. Her luggage was—somewhere else, and she was a day later than planned, cutting it so close that she'd ended up finding funeral attire in a shop in the Amsterdam airport. The long-sleeved, jersey dress was simple and unadorned. Perhaps not as nice as she'd have chosen had she had any time to prepare, but beggars couldn't be choosers. At least it was the appropriate color.

Kennedy didn't recognize any of the vehicles in the drive. And why should she? She'd left this place at eighteen and hadn't come back. In that time, they could have made a thousand and one changes and she wouldn't have been any the wiser. Would it still feel like home without Mom here to fill it with her big, boisterous personality? Heart in her throat, Kennedy climbed the steps. The third one still squeaked. That tiny, familiar detail made her ache. At the door, she hesitated, wondering if she should knock or ring the bell of this place that had once been hers. Deciding that smacked too much of cowardice, she tried the knob. It turned beneath her hand, and she stepped inside.

Her irrational fear that everything had changed abated as she took in the living room. Same overstuffed sofas. Same gallery of pictures. Kennedy even recognized some of the tchotchkes she'd sent her mom over the years, set around for decoration. The omnipresent scent of her mother's coffee and the low murmur of voices pulled her toward the kitchen and the center of the home she'd left so long ago. Kennedy didn't realize how much she'd expected Joan to be seated at the big farmhouse table, hands wrapped around one of her favorite mugs, until the sight of the empty chair sucker punched her in the gut, ripping right through the emotional numbness of exhaustion.

"Well, look who decided to grace us with her presence."

At the acerbic tone, Kennedy looked over at her sister Athena. She stood by the counter, her long brown hair caught up in the same utilitarian bun Kennedy knew she wore daily to keep it out of the way in her restaurant kitchen. Kennedy didn't brook offense at the hard set of Athena's jaw and the glint in her dry eyes. She well knew Athena didn't do upset. She didn't cry. She got pissed and bit at whoever the most convenient target happened to be. Her kitchen staff had probably been on the receiving end of a fit worthy of Gordon Ramsey when she got the news about Joan.

"Enough. We'll have none of that today." Maggie, the middle Reynolds daughter and a year younger than Kennedy, looked calm and in control in her neat black suit, her pale blonde hair pulled back in a tidy chignon, with a strand of pearls at her throat. The very picture of the consummate professional woman she'd become.

"You made it." Pru hurried over, immediately enfolding Kennedy in a hug that had the tears threatening again. "I was beginning to worry."

She fought for control, hanging on to Pru for all she was worth. "So was I. My luggage may end up in Sri Lanka, but I'm here."

"Have you eaten?" Pru asked.

The very thought of food made Kennedy's stomach turn. "Can't."

"Coffee, then." Without waiting for an answer, Pru went to pour her a mug.

Not knowing what else to do, Kennedy set her carry-on down and dropped her purse.

Maggie hesitated, something rippling over her face before she crossed the room and folded Kennedy into a hug. It wasn't so long or warm as Pru's, but it was so much more than Kennedy had expected. Of all of her sisters, Maggie had the most reason to hate her.

"The car will be here in a couple of hours to pick us up."

Another car, this one to the very last place Kennedy wanted to go. But there was no running or hiding from this. Accepting the coffee, she asked, "So what's the plan?"

"Visitation at Kavanaugh's from one to two, then a graveside service," Maggie explained.

"After that, it's back here for food. We're expecting a big crowd. A lot of Mom's fosters are coming in, thanks to Xander," Pru said. "He made all the calls."

Kennedy considered it a minor miracle she didn't choke on her coffee. Something akin to panic crawled up her spine and shot her heart rate through the roof. Of course Xander Kincaid was still in Eden's Ridge. Exactly where his father thought he was supposed to be. Why should that have changed?

But she hadn't prepared herself for the possibility of seeing him. Not really. Her entire focus had been on getting home for the funeral. Consciously deepening her breath, she worked to slow her heart and tamp down the anxiety, keeping her tone even. "That was kind of him. I'm sure everyone wants to pay their respects."

Why, exactly, was Xander helping her sister out with funeral arrangements? Wasn't that the kind of thing you did for a significant other?

And why should you care? You walked away and gave up any right to feel jealousy over who Xander's with. But the chiding did nothing to stem the quick prick of resentment at the idea that he'd moved on to her sister, of all people. Pru was exactly the kind of woman Xander needed. Rooted here and focused on home and hearth. Not a screw up with itchy feet and no plan for the future. Any guy would be lucky to have her.

"Kennedy?"

How long had Pru been speaking? "What?"

"Bless your heart, I know you're exhausted. I said there's time for you to grab a shower, if you want. I know you've been on the go for a few days now."

That probably meant she looked as bad as she felt. There was only so much she could do to make herself presentable in an airport bathroom or service station. "A shower would be great."

"I've put you in your old room. There are fresh towels in the cabinet in the bathroom. I'm sure we can…" She trailed off as the slow, mournful notes of Beethoven's "Moonlight Sonata" began to sound. "Ari."

They all listened in silence as the girl poured out her grief at the piano, wringing every last drop of emotion from the instrument. Joan had said the child was gifted, but Kennedy had never imagined this. Tears spilled down her cheeks as the music shattered the last vestiges of her control, unleashing the devastation she'd pushed to the side just to get here. By the time the last note faded, they were all crying, save Athena, who looked ready to punch something.

Pru wiped at her eyes. "It's the first time she's left her room in three days. I think she's afraid that if she leaves the house, social services will take her away."

Maggie went ramrod straight. "Have they threatened to?"

"No. Mae knows this is devastating. She's not going to rock the boat right now. So I'm her guardian until something more permanent can be decided on."

"Permanent like what?" Athena asked.

Pru shrugged. "I don't know. I think Mae's been putting out feelers to see if she can track down Ari's birth parents. She didn't have any luck when Sofia—Ari's grandmother—passed away, but with this… She doesn't want to leave any stone unturned."

"Poor kid," Athena muttered. "No wonder she's terrified."

As Beethoven rolled into Debussy, Kennedy tried to imagine what she'd have done in Ari's shoes. Her mother had taken off when Kennedy was only seven. Her dad had done his best for a while, taking her on the road in his eighteen wheeler as he trucked across country. But even he'd given up on the parenting gig after a while, announcing that it'd been a good run, but it just wasn't working anymore. She'd been twelve when he dumped her into the system, nearly thirteen by the time she'd come to Joan, saddled with the kiss-of-death moniker of "troubled." If there'd been even a whiff of a possibility that they'd send her back to her father, she wouldn't have hesitated before bolting.

"We have to do something." Kennedy wiped at her own eyes. "We have to make her feel safe and protected, like Mom did. We all know what it feels like to have the rug pulled out from under us. She has enough to deal with without adding worry that she's going to get thrown back into the system. We have to look after her. It's what Mom would've wanted."

Athena turned from the window. "You're hardly in a position to know what Mom wanted."

Kennedy absorbed the blow, biting back the protest that rose in her throat. She was too tired to fight with Athena. Too tired to fight with any of them. And what could she really say? She hadn't been here. That none of them knew the true reason why hardly mattered. She still couldn't explain. The fact was, it had been a risk coming back here, even now.

"Kennedy's not wrong," Maggie said. "Mom considered Ari another daughter. The fact that the legal paperwork didn't get finished before she died was just a formality. That makes her our sister. And that means we fight for her."

A little of the tension leeched away. They'd fight. So sayeth Maggie. Nothing short of God himself would dare go against her.

"There will be time to figure it out after today," Pru said. "The music's stopped. Maybe she'll finally eat something. I'll go see."

Feeling raw and wanting some space, Kennedy scooped up her carry-on and purse. "I'm gonna get that shower now."

~

XANDER CONSIDERED it an honor to lead the procession to Joan's final resting place. The line of cars snaked down the mountain, filling multiple switchbacks. The cemetery was an older one, high up on the ridge where you could look out over the Great Smoky Mountains. She'd loved those mountains all her life, and he thought it fitting that she be laid to rest with such a view. He hoped that when her daughters came to visit the graveside—if they came to visit after today—they'd find some comfort in that.

Stepping out of his cruiser, Xander looked toward the car parked behind the hearse. The doors opened and the sisters slid out, all in unrelieved black. Pru, Maggie, and Athena he'd seen, already offered his condolences. Kennedy was the last one out. He wanted to be cool and unaffected, wanted to hang on to the bitterness and anger over her abandonment. And it was there, as it had been for years. But even at this distance, he could see the signs of weeping, and he couldn't harden his heart. Not fully. His ribs felt too tight, and he couldn't take a full breath.

She'd grown up. He'd known that objectively. He certainly had in the last ten years. But he'd worked hard not to imagine her as a woman, not to wonder how she'd changed, so in his mind, she'd stayed the fresh-faced girl of eighteen. Grief and exhaustion did little to dim her beauty. She was a knockout, with a subtle edge of...something. A confidence he didn't remember from high school, as if she was comfortable in her own skin now. Or as comfortable as she could be under the circumstances.

Not trusting himself to maintain the necessary emotional distance, Xander stuck to keeping physical space between them, busying himself by directing the parking lineup of all the mourners as the pall bearers gathered at the rear of the hearse. They were all former fosters of Joan's, now men grown and off on their own. Xander had heard their stories, and dozens of others, when he'd called to break the news of her passing. With only a few exceptions, every single person on Joan's list had returned to say goodbye and pay their respects to the woman who'd changed their lives. Between them and all of her many friends from Eden's Ridge, the graveside was packed.

At the direction of the funeral home staff, everyone gathered in neat rows around the plot, careful not to trip over the artificial turf covering the grim reality of a freshly dug grave. Tensions between the sisters were evident as they stood at the edge. Their postures were stiff, no hands or arms linked in support. So different from growing up, when they'd been a unit. But even as Xander crossed over to join the crowd, the four of them closed ranks around Ari, taking her hand or touching her shoulder. The Reynolds sisters might be a family divided, but they were still a family at the heart. Joan had forged those links, and he thought the child would be the one to reinforce them.

Pastor Hodgson began the service, his booming baritone carrying across the cemetery as he spoke of a life cut tragically short. "Joan Reynolds was a good woman, a good Christian, who believed in healing the world through love. After spending fifteen years working as a social worker and being frustrated with the limitations in her ability to help the children on her caseload, she left that job and opened her home as a foster parent. She spent the next twenty-five years devoting her life to that endeavor, impacting the lives of more than a hundred children—none more so than her daughters."

The minister rolled on through the service, offering prayers and platitudes. When, at last, he lapsed into silence, heads bowed in respect, in mourning. Then a single, tremulous voice lifted in song. Kennedy. Eyes closed, face raised to the sky, she sang, gaining strength with every word. After a few bars, Xander recognized the lyrics to "Bridge Over Troubled Water." Raw and unaccompanied, the sound of it sent chills down his spine, stripping away the hurt and resentment, until all he wanted was to comfort and soothe. Because she was aching, and no matter what had passed between them or how it had ended, a part of him still needed to protect her.

She was weeping by the end, tears streaming down her cheeks and sobs stealing her breath for the final lines. Pru took her hand. Maggie looped an arm through hers. Even Athena reached out to squeeze her shoulder. In this, at least, it seemed they could put aside their differences.

Pastor Hodgson made a few more remarks. And then it was done. Each of the sisters stepped forward to lay a single white rose over the polished coffin before slowly stepping away. Kennedy pressed a hand to the wood, chin quivering. Then she, too, stepped away.

Mourners moved in clumps toward parked cars. They would, Xander knew, be heading back to the house for the reception. He'd told himself he wasn't going, that he didn't want to add to the strain with his presence. Pru, at least, would worry about him and Kennedy being in the same room again after all this time. Who knew whether Kennedy herself would be bothered? But Porter had made it up for the funeral after all, and Xander didn't want to pass up the opportunity to see one of his oldest friends. And, for better or worse, a part of him wanted to see Kennedy, just to check on her.

By the time he arrived, the house was packed. It might've looked like a party but for the quiet murmur of voices and the lack of music. People already had plates of food and visited in clusters of three or four. Porter Ingram stood across the living room, hands jammed in the pockets of his suit, scanning the gallery of photos, much as Xander had done the other day.

"A lot of memories here," Xander murmured.

Porter turned and offered a small smile. "Yeah." He opened his arms, and Xander returned the back thumping hug.

"Glad you could make it. How's Gatlinburg?"

When wildfires had broken out in November, Porter had headed south as part of the National Guard to try to contain the blaze. The aftermath had left Gatlinburg ravaged and burned more than a hundred thousand acres across eight states. In the face of the devastation, he'd stayed as part of the reconstruction efforts.

"It's going. We're starting to see some solid progress, but it'll be a long damned time before the land heals. The Ridge was damned lucky the fires didn't make it this far."

Xander gave thanks for that every day. "Are you here long?"

"Have to head back tonight. We're at a critical stage in the project just now, and I've got to be on site tomorrow."

"Got time for a beer before you go?"

"Depends what time I finish up here." Porter sighed. "Can't believe this, man. Joan was a force of nature. It just seems so senseless."

"It is senseless."

They both turned at the quiet voice.

"Maggie."

Xander wondered if she noticed the softening in Porter's expression and tone.

She'd lost the suit jacket since the cemetery but looked no less professional in the slim skirt and blouse, all that pale blonde hair gathered in a roll at her nape. Xander imagined she dressed much the same for the boardroom or her high-powered clients in LA. He wasn't sure exactly what she did for a living except that it used that terrifying brain of hers.

"It's Margaret these days."

"Old habits die hard," Porter replied.

Maggie winced. "Well, I suppose it's better than Mudbug."

"I was fifteen and stupid."

Porter had been fifteen and in love with her, Xander knew. Not that Porter had ever felt comfortable acting on it while living under the same roof.

"Brother's prerogative, I guess." She laid a hand on his arm. "Thank you for coming."

"Of course."

They both watched as she moved on to greet other guests.

"Brother," Porter grumbled.

"So that's still the way the wind blows, huh?"

Porter twitched his broad shoulders in irritation. "Doesn't matter. She'll be headed back to California soon enough." But his eyes followed her as she circulated the room. "Let's go get some food."

Athena had taken over in the kitchen, overseeing the spread of food with a surly air that didn't invite conversation. The big farmhouse table groaned under the weight of all the dishes, and Xander had no doubt more would be forthcoming from those who hadn't yet been by. Pru fussed by the stove, making more iced tea. Catching sight of him, she shot a panicked look toward the back door. Following her gaze, saw Kennedy picking her way across the lawn.

At the table, Porter held out a plate.

"I'll get some in a bit. I need to do something first."

"Xander." Hands knitted, Pru stepped in front of the door.

He wrapped his arm around her shoulders and pressed a kiss to her temple. "I'm just going to check on her. That's all." Before she could protest further, he slipped outside to follow.

Xander had no idea what he was going to say. Some dim part of him knew this was probably a bad idea, but he could no more stay away from her than a moth could a flame—even knowing he was likely to get burned. But she wasn't alone down at the overlook. Ari sat on the long bench set beneath the spreading branches of an oak. Xander stopped, wondering whether he should head on back inside.

"I always used to like to come out here to think when I lived here." Kennedy's voice floated back on the faint breeze as she sat. She didn't touch the girl, didn't encroach on her personal space. They both just sat, looking out toward the lowering sun. In another hour it'd be full dark.

"You don't have to talk," she continued. "I know you're sad and scared, and I know you don't really know me. But I just wanted to say that I'm here for you, if you ever want to talk. Sometimes talking helps you feel less alone."

Ari looked over at her for a long moment before turning her gaze back to the mountains. "That was nice, what you did today."

Kennedy's only acknowledgment that the girl had just spoken for the first time in almost a week was to glance over. "What was?"

"The singing. When my *abuela* died, the priest did the service, but there was no music. Only prayers. Joan would've liked it."

Kennedy's shoulders rose and fell, and her voice, when she spoke, was a little choked. "Simon and Garfunkel were particular favorites of hers. But she loved all kinds of music. At one point, we had so many kids in the house who sang or played some kind of an instrument, we put together a band."

"Yeah?"

She gave a watery laugh. "Oh, we were absolutely terrible. But Joan sat and listened to our concerts like we were The Beatles or something." She hesitated. "Do you even know who The Beatles are at your age?"

Ari shook her head and leaned against Kennedy's shoulder. "You could maybe show me."

Kennedy wrapped an arm around her, tugging her close. "I will absolutely do that."

Ari needed this way more than Xander needed…whatever it was he'd hoped to get out of this encounter. Edging back, he made his way quietly back to the house.

CHAPTER 3

𝒦ENNEDY WAS STILL HUNG over from tears and jet lag as she and her sisters stepped into the attorney's office the day after the funeral. The drive to Johnson City had been a blur, but at least there'd been coffee—Athena's doing, so it'd been excellent. Maggie gave their name to the fifty-something receptionist, and in a matter of minutes, the four of them were escorted into an office full of leather and wood and law books.

The attorney, Robert Barth, came around his desk, offering a hand to each of them in turn.

"Thank you for coming to the service yesterday," Pru said.

Kennedy fixed her attention on the man as she shook hands, noting the receding black hair, the faint paunch beneath his well-cut suit. He was close to forty, with laugh lines around his brown eyes. She had no memory of seeing him at the funeral. Then again, a stampede of elephants could've trooped through and she probably would've missed it. Her entire focus had been on Ari, her sisters, and that dreadful, dark hole in the ground.

"I would've been happy to come to the house."

"We thought it best to handle things here," Maggie said.

"Of course, of course. As you wish." Robert gestured toward a small conference table surrounded by six, low-backed leather chairs. "Please, sit. Can I have Marlene make you some coffee? Tea?"

Maggie and Athena declined. Pru asked for coffee. Kennedy would've given her right arm for a properly-steeped cup of Irish breakfast tea, but she figured that the best on offer here would be weak tea bags, so she demurred as well, grabbing a chair at random and sinking in.

After rummaging around his desk for a moment, Robert came to join them. "I still can't believe she's gone. You know, I was one of her first fosters?"

Pru jolted. "Oh? I didn't realize."

"It's been a long, long time. I was with her for about nine months, while my mother went through rehab and got her life back together."

"You were able to go home again?" Athena asked.

"I was."

"Lucky," she murmured.

Kennedy wanted to reach out a hand to her sister. Athena hadn't been able to go home, and she'd never fully gotten over it. But at the opposite end of the table, Athena was out of reach. She wouldn't have appreciated the gesture anyway.

"Joan always kept tabs on me," Robert continued, smiling a bit in memory. "Came to my high school, college, and law school graduations. She gave me my first briefcase. Anyway, I've been handling her legal affairs ever since."

Memory lane. Everybody at the reception yesterday had wanted to walk down it, share their story for how Joan had come into their lives, how she'd improved it. There were so, so many stories. The fact that there'd be no more made Kennedy heartsick. The world wasn't ready to do without her. Kennedy wasn't ready to do without her.

Evidently sensing they were ready to get down to business,

Robert cleared his throat and unfolded the papers in his hand. "Joan had me draw up her will years ago, with modifications as each of you were formally adopted. I'll just read it through, then address any questions you may have."

He launched in. By the second line of legalese, Kennedy was already tuning out. She'd always had a crappy attention span, especially for things that had unnecessarily formal or complicated language. It was part of the reason she'd done so poorly in school. If not for Pru and Maggie, the chances of her graduating at all would've been pretty slim. College hadn't even been on her radar, and she'd much preferred all the hands-on learning she'd done over the past ten years. Still, none of that had adequately prepared her to understand any of this.

Realizing Robert had finished reading, Kennedy struggled to focus. "I'm sorry. I'm having a little trouble concentrating. Could you sum that up in plain English?"

"Of course. She's bequeathed a lengthy and specific list of items to you and your sisters, as well as various other friends or former fosters. I'll certainly provide you with that list. As you know, y'all are her only family, so the house and acreage it sits on, as well as the trust that has covered most of the upkeep on the property, is left to the four of you, equally. The property has been in Reynolds hands since the mid-1800s, so she was very clear that it go to y'all."

So home would remain home. That was good.

"What about the lien?" Maggie asked.

"Lien?" Kennedy asked.

"A few years ago, the house needed some significant repairs. Mom took out a sizable loan against the property to do it. At that time, there was no reason to think she wouldn't be around to see that it was fully paid off before we inherited."

"Wouldn't the trust cover that?" Athena asked.

"She didn't want to pull that much out at that time." Maggie shrugged. "It was her decision. I didn't question it."

"Officially, the estate will go into probate until any debts are settled," Robert explained. "Depending on how complicated things are, that can take anywhere from a few months to years."

"Does that mean the house just sits until things are settled?" Pru asked, aghast.

"There's no reason you can't continue to use the house, if that's what you want. Another option would be to sell the property. That would satisfy the debt outright."

"No." They all but shouted it in unison.

Robert smiled. "Glad to hear it. As executor, I'll obtain a current copy of all the loan paperwork, find out the outstanding balance, and the like. And I'll follow up on everything else to do with Joan's estate—her retirement accounts, life insurance, the trust, and other assets, etc.—to see that things are settled as easily as possible and with as little fuss for you as necessary. And, of course, I'll keep you apprised every step of the way."

"So, if we want to keep the property, we have to see that the lien is paid, correct?" Maggie asked.

"At the end of it all, yes."

"Okay. Then we need to make a plan that enables us to do that, and to manage upkeep on the place, as well as property taxes, etc."

Kennedy had no idea how they'd do such a thing, especially as they weren't all actually staying in Eden's Ridge. She couldn't see Maggie leaving LA or Athena walking away from her Michelin-starred restaurant in Chicago. And even if she herself stayed, what help could she really be? She didn't have Maggie's business mind or Pru's deep connection to the community or even Athena's drive. All she had to offer was a strong back and a willingness to pitch in however she could. She just hoped it would be enough.

"With the probate, you have time to sort it out," Robert assured them.

Well, thank God for that. "What about Ari?" Kennedy asked. "Are there any provisions for her in the will?"

With a look of regret, Robert shook his head. "I know she intended to add her once the adoption was finalized, but it didn't get that far. I'm afraid her fate is in the hands of the state."

"We'll add it to the agenda for the family meeting," Maggie said. She gathered her coat. "We appreciate everything Robert. If you'll forward me copies of all the financials to go over as you get them, I'd be much obliged."

"Happy to."

He passed on copies of the list so they could begin locating and distributing assorted mementos to their respective recipients. And then they were out of the office, back into the chilly March sunshine.

"I'm glad that's over," Athena said.

Mouth set in a grim line, Maggie just shook her head. "It's only just beginning."

~

"I HEARD down at the Snort and Curl she still has a voice like an angel." The voice of Esther Vaughn, administrative assistant and dispatch for the Stone County Sheriff's Office—definitely *not* an angel—echoed through the air duct to where Xander was just shutting the back door of the building.

At the sound of it, the nagging headache throbbing behind his eyes ratcheted up a notch. If the beauty shop was already talking about Kennedy's return, it was only a matter of time before he started getting harassed about it. He wasn't in the mood. His sleep had been interrupted to take a call about a prowler skulking around Elvira's Tavern at two in the morning. The prowler had turned out to be a bear digging through the dumpster out back. By the time Xander had made it home again, he couldn't go back to sleep.

"A damned shame about her mama." This from Jarvis Riley, their jail administrator. He'd been a few years ahead of Xander in school.

"Wait, now. Who is this woman?" Chief Investigator Leanne Hammond. The new girl.

Essie sighed in that way Xander had seen her do over the romance novels she kept in her desk for lulls. He knew where this was going, so he quickened his pace and strode into what constituted the bullpen, glaring at the cluster of his coworkers. "She's talking about my high school girlfriend. Because, in case you haven't figured it out in the last six months, not enough happens around here for people to talk about more current events."

"Kennedy's back in town after how long? That *is* a current event," Jarvis argued.

"The last thing she's thinking about is me." *And hey, that's par for the course. At least she has a good reason this time.*

"You've seen her then?" Essie asked, not looking in the least embarrassed about being caught gossiping about him.

"You know I was at the funeral yesterday." Though seeing her at a distance probably wasn't what Essie was fishing for.

"How did she look?"

Sad and lost and so fragile, a stiff wind might've broken her. "Like she'd just lost her mother," Xander snapped. His tone of rebuke had absolutely no effect.

"You know that's not what I meant," Essie said.

"I know what you meant," he gritted out. "This is not a social visit. Not a return to the Ridge for some happy occasion, where we sat around and shot the shit, talking about the good times. Her world's just been turned upside down. And I'm sure as soon as the fallout is sorted, she'll be off to Venezuela or Greece or New Zealand or wherever the hell the wind blows her. Again." Xander heard the bitterness in his voice and couldn't seem to stop it.

"I gather you were the dumpee in this scenario," Leanne said.

"Brilliant deduction. So glad you're our Chief Investigator."

His snarl didn't faze her in the least. "What happened?"

"I'm sure if you head on down to the Snort and Curl, they'll be more than happy to fill you in, since nobody has enough going on in their lives to talk about something else."

Essie opened her mouth, as if to save Leanne the trip.

"Don't y'all all have work? 'Cause if you don't, I'm sure I can come up with more paperwork," the sheriff boomed.

Just fucking perfect.

But they all suddenly found something else to do.

"Xander, see you in my office?"

"Yes, sir." With one last glare, he took the save, shutting the door to the office behind him, as was expected.

"So Kennedy came home after all," Buck said conversationally.

"Her mother *died.* Of course she came home." Having seen her, he couldn't quite believe he'd doubted she would for a moment.

"How are you feeling about all this, son?"

Xander leveled his father with a flat stare. "What? We're gonna talk about feelings? Really?"

Buck had never liked Kennedy, and he'd made no secret of the fact that he was glad she left. She'd been the only thing he and Xander had ever really disagreed on.

"She walked away from you without a word all those years ago. There's no shame or surprise in having some unresolved… stuff about it."

"Stuff," Xander repeated. Well, that was one word for it.

After two glorious years together, they'd been on top of the world, full of excitement and plans to see the world—or as much of it as they could fit in after graduation. Being a practical sort, Xander had thought they should work through the summer and build up a little bit of cash before they left. She'd agreed. Then, graduation night they'd had a huge fight. He'd been drunk and stupid and said things he didn't quite remember. But he remembered enough to know he owed her a huge apology when he sobered up. Except when he'd showed up at her house the next day, he discovered she'd bailed on him, leaving town without a word. He'd been devastated.

Xander wished he was too manly to admit that, but she'd gutted him. And by God, he wanted answers from her. Ten years later and he was still pissed, still hurt that he'd had no chance to apologize, to explain himself. But seeing her again yesterday, there'd been other "stuff" there, too. He didn't want to think about the other stuff, and he sure as hell didn't want to talk about it with his dad.

"I can assure you there's no stuff. I'm not some lovesick puppy in danger of being led astray. Kennedy settled things between us years ago, and that's the end of it. No matter how much people around here insist on gossiping to the contrary." It was a partial truth. She'd ended it. He planned to settle it now and get his answers before she left again for parts unknown. She owed him that much.

Something in Buck's face relaxed. Relief at not actually being forced to go through with the feelings talk? "Glad to hear it. If you were going to cast your eye on a Reynolds, you'd do better with Pru. Now there's a fine woman."

"Don't even go there, Dad. Pru's like my sister. Always has been."

"Too bad. Your mama and I always liked her."

Xander bristled at the reminder that his parents—or at least his father—had never approved of Kennedy. Xander had never cared, but she'd wanted so desperately to be accepted by his family. It had always felt cruel that they'd denied her that. And why did he even still care? They were both grown adults, neither of whom needed his parents—or anyone else's—approval.

Old habits, he decided. "Was there something you actually needed? Or was this just some attempt to play Dr. Phil?"

"Got some process papers that need delivering today."

Thank God. He was ready to get back to doing his actual job. "Okay then. Who and where?"

CHAPTER 4

"I DON'T KNOW WHY we're here," Pru said. "We've still got enough casseroles to get us through the end of the month."

Kennedy grabbed a shopping cart and headed toward the produce aisle. "Because woman cannot live on casseroles alone, even in Tennessee. If I don't have some vegetables that aren't globbed in cheese or wrapped in bacon, my arteries are going to clog in a week. Plus, I need to pick up some basic toiletries and stuff since my luggage still hasn't arrived." She'd have to pick up some clothes, too, if it didn't show up soon.

"You realize you've just blasphemed, right? Bacon and cheese are their own food groups here. Or had you forgotten?"

"I hadn't forgotten. But my tolerance is down after all the time away." Plus she'd wanted an excuse to get out of the house and away from the tension.

Maggie had sequestered herself with copies of the financial records Robert sent over the day before. Whatever the news, it wasn't good. Athena was pacing the place like a caged jungle cat, itching to get back to Olympus and knowing she couldn't leave Eden's Ridge yet. And Pru was fretting over Ari, who still wasn't saying or eating much. She'd gone back to school this morning. They were all expecting a call for an early pick up. A grocery run seemed the easiest way to get a brief escape and distract Pru.

"Well, since we're here, I'm gonna go grab some ice cream." Pru made a beeline for the freezer section.

"Far be it for me to deny you the comfort of Ben and Jerry."

As her sister wandered off, Kennedy swept through the personal care aisle, picking up the necessities before heading over to produce. She browsed the fresh veggies, adding potatoes, carrots, and onions to the cart, then grabbing some apples and the fixings for spinach salads. Wondering if there was a chance in hell the butcher had any lamb in the meat department, she circled onto the canned goods aisle.

"I ran into Porter at the funeral. He said progress down in Gatlinburg is going really well, so the resort might reopen this summer."

Kennedy stopped in the middle of the aisle. She knew that voice. A part of her had been waiting to hear it from the moment she'd set foot back in the Ridge. He'd been at the funeral? She'd wondered why she hadn't seen him. Wondered if he'd made himself scarce to avoid her.

Hands gripping the cart like a lifeline, she slowly made her way down the aisle and eased around the end to peer down the next row. And there he was, big as life. She couldn't see his face, but she'd know him anywhere. Xander Kincaid. The reason she'd stayed away all these years. And why she'd always wanted to come back.

Feigning nonchalance, she reached for whatever was on the display at the end of the aisle, taking the chance to study him. His brown hair was considerably shorter now, no longer curling over his collar. His khaki shirt stretched across shoulders that were broader than they'd been at eighteen, and he still had the best backside in Stone County. A duty belt hung around his hips. So her former bad boy had become a lawman exactly like his father always wanted. Looked like Buck had been right after all. She'd been a bad influence.

How long had it taken him to fall in line after she'd left? A week? A month? Or had he made it the whole summer? Had he ever really loved her at all? Maybe she'd just been a diversion for the hometown boy who'd never really had any intention of leaving.

Feeling foolish, Kennedy tried to shrug off the disappointment. It was ancient history. She should finish grabbing supplies, round up Pru, and get out of here before he saw her. Realizing it was a box of stuffing mix she'd picked up, she reached to put it back. The zipper of her hoodie caught on the buggy, yanking it into the endcap display with a crash that echoed through the store and sent several boxes of stuffing tumbling to the floor.

Of course Xander turned around and looked right at her.

Crap.

Heart pounding, Kennedy immediately unsnagged her hoodie and crouched down to pick up the boxes. She had three in her hands when a pair of black, lace-up boots stepped into her field of view. Their owner squatted down and reached for some of the boxes.

"Why are you even looking at this stuff? You hate stuffing."

"Perhaps a better question is why they're highlighting it in March. Hello, Xander." She made herself look at him. None of the softness of youth lingered around that chiseled jaw. The rest of him had clearly transitioned from the last traces of boy into man. But his mouth. His mouth was as she'd remembered, those sculpted lips just barely curved at the edge of a ready smile.

She hadn't expected the possibility of a smile from him. Her breath quickened at his nearness and her fingers itched to trace those lips. Would he taste the same? Needing a moment to get her own reaction under control, Kennedy turned to put the boxes back on the display.

Xander did the same before rocking back on his heels, all traces of the smile gone. "I'm sorry about your mama."

"Thank you."

Cue awkward silence. What was she supposed to say to this man she'd once planned a life with?

"How's everybody holding up?" Xander asked.

"As well as can be expected, I guess. I keep walking into rooms thinking she'll be there. The house just feels *wrong* without her in it."

"I bet. We all felt like that when you left."

The barb struck true. Kennedy opened her mouth. Closed it again. What could she say to that?

I didn't want to leave you!

Even if she were free to admit the truth, it was too little, too late for that. She'd chosen to protect him, and that was a choice she'd have to continue to live with.

"Xander!" Pru hurried down the aisle and right on into the middle of the awkward. "I wanted to thank you again for all your help last week." She moved into him and his arms went around her in an easy, affectionate hug.

"Of course. You know I'd do anything for you."

The nip of jealousy was quick as a mosquito. Kennedy slapped it down, feeling stupid. Xander and Pru were friends. They'd been friends since they were children. And if they were more now, they had every right to be. Especially since apparently none of them thought she'd ever come back.

And you haven't until now, so they weren't wrong.

"You may regret that offer," Pru warned, stepping back. "Depending on what happens with the house."

His brows drew together in concern. "What's going on with the house?"

"Mom took out a big loan to make some major repairs."

"Yeah, about three years ago. I remember when Delbert Monroe put on that new roof. Is there a problem with it?"

"Maggie's sorting through the details, but the bottom line is we have to figure out how to pay off the loan in order to keep the property. It's the only stable home Ari's ever had other than that stint with her grandmother."

Given her background, stability was paramount to Pru. And maybe that was why, of all of them, she'd never left once she settled in Eden's Ridge. Which made her absolutely the best one of them to be in charge of Ari right now.

Kennedy wrapped an arm around her shoulders. "We're going to come up with something. We all know Maggie's a genius. It will be all right."

Pru just grimaced. "That's easy for you to say. You won't have to deal with whatever it is when you go back to Ireland or wherever."

She absorbed the slap of that. This was Pru's automatic thought? And not just hers. Awareness of Xander's censorious look scraped along Kennedy's skin. He totally believed she'd bail on her family in the middle of this crapstorm. And why wouldn't he think that after what she'd done to him? Why wouldn't any of them think that?

A bitter, helpless rage rose up inside her, almost choking her in its potency. She'd forever be judged because of a mistake they didn't even know she'd made. This was the purgatory she'd been sentenced to a decade ago. She was so damned tired of having everything ruined because of that one night. She'd lost Xander, lost her family in all but the most peripheral sense. She'd thought she'd made her peace with that. But being back here, seeing exactly how bad the rift was between her and her sisters, made her want to fight as she hadn't been brave enough to do at eighteen. Maybe Flynn was right and it was time to stop running.

Taking a firm grip on her temper and ignoring the judgment coming off Xander in waves, Kennedy kept her attention on Pru. "I'm not going back."

Surprise flickered over Xander's face. Kennedy ignored that too.

"You're not?" Pru's hopeful expression sliced her through the gut.

"I called a friend this morning to pack up and ship the rest of my things home from Kerry." Which, okay, she hadn't done. Yet. But she would as soon as they got back to the house. "I'm not leaving you to deal with all this alone."

Pru's eyes watered.

"Oh God, don't cry. We've all cried oceans the past week."

Pru hugged her. "Shut up. I'm allowed to cry when my sister finally comes home."

Guilt knocked hard against Kennedy's breast bone, and she couldn't stop herself from looking at Xander over her sister's shoulder. But it wasn't condemnation she saw in his eyes. It was...curiosity.

No. Oh no. She knew him. Once he started wondering about something, he was like a dog with a bone. He'd keep worrying at it until he figured it out. She had to get out of here because it was only a matter of time before he came around demanding answers she couldn't give him.

"We should get on home," Kennedy urged. "I'd like to be there in case Ari needs a pick up."

"You're right. Xander, I'll see you later. And thank your mama again for the enchiladas."

He wrapped an arm around Pru and gave her another squeeze. "I know you've still got your hands full, so if you need anything, just ask."

She smiled. "You're the best."

He made no move to touch Kennedy. As they made their way to the checkout, she told herself that was for the best. She didn't need any reminders of what it felt like to be pressed up against him. There couldn't be anything between them now, and she had plenty of mental fodder for torture without adding that to the mix. If she was truly moving home, she had to find a way to coexist with him in some kind of platonic-acquaintance way.

Still, as they loaded bags into the back of Pru's car, Kennedy couldn't stop herself from asking, "So you and Xander, huh?"

Pru stared at her with a blank expression. "Me and Xander what?"

Oh God, was she really going to make her spell it out?

"Together?" Pru laughed. "Oh, honey no. He's like my brother." She sobered, laying a hand on Kennedy's arm. "And even if he wasn't, I wouldn't do that to you."

The relief that flooded through her was appalling. In defense, she jerked her shoulders in a shrug. "It's no big deal if you did. We were a long time ago. Just kids." Kids who'd done naked things, but kids nonetheless.

Pru grabbed on to her other arm in a half embrace. "No. Never."

Kennedy fought the urge to shrug off the touch and the expression of gentle understanding. "Just thought I should check so I didn't stick my foot in it. Let's go home."

∼

BY DAY'S END, Xander's patience was at an all-time low. He'd have given a great deal for one of those calls about loose livestock that would've taken him to the ass end of the county for hours at a time. But no. He'd been inside the Ridge proper and one call after another—from traffic stops to vandalism to welfare checks—every-damn-body in town was asking him about Kennedy. Which meant he hadn't been able to stop thinking about her for longer than five minutes since their encounter this morning. He just wanted a beer and an uncomplicated hour watching the latest basketball game in the March Madness tournament with his best friend. Logan Maxwell was a transplant to Eden's Ridge, so he wouldn't have the million questions all the locals did. Thank God.

With that in mind, Xander tugged open the door to Elvira's Tavern and stepped inside. He scanned the space, already noting a few locals who liked to over-indulge on a regular basis and a couple on the far side he was expecting a domestic disturbance call on any day now. He nodded a greeting to the various patrons who waved. Logan had beat him here and currently occupied a stool at the bar. Across from him, her tray tucked under one arm, was Trish Morgan. She leaned conspiratorially toward Logan, her generous cleavage on display in the tight Elvira's t-shirt. Please, dear God, let him not be in the mood tonight. Xander needed some guy time, not to play wingman.

"Everybody expected him to blow up, but he was nice as could be, right there in the grocery store."

Xander stopped dead in his tracks and gave serious consideration to just turning right back around and heading home. But he was out of beer at home, and he hadn't picked any up when he'd been at Garden of Eden this morning. Setting his teeth, he stepped up to the bar.

"Do people really think I'm enough of an asshole to tell her off when her mama just died?"

Trish straightened, plunking a hand down on one hip and giving the same toss of her hair she'd been giving since she was a cheerleader back in high school. "Of course not. Your mama would've tanned your hide. But it would've been understandable if you had...all things considered."

Denver Hershal, lumbered over from the other end of the bar. "We're short-handed and you got tables." The beefy bartender crossed his tattooed arms and gave a pointed look across the restaurant.

With a sassy salute, Trish sashayed off to deal with them.

"Thanks," Xander muttered.

"No problem. Usual?"

Given the pounding behind his eyes, Xander was pretty sure a Corona wasn't going to cut it, but when you were one of only a few cops in town, you were never really off duty, so the one beer it was. He nodded and turned to Logan. "Get a table?"

"Sure. I could eat."

Xander scooped up the longneck Denver set out for him, and they made their way to a table in the corner. It was in the shadows, with a decent enough view of one of the flat-screens playing the game.

As soon as they were settled, Trish was by the table. "Y'all eatin'?"

He and Logan exchanged a glance. "Loaded fries and an onion bomb."

"Comin' right up."

She headed for the kitchen, and Xander settled back in his chair, lifting the beer to his lips and checking out the score.

"So you finally saw her."

Xander bristled. "Not you, too."

"Can't blame me for being curious, man. This whole town's talking about her being back and waiting for some kind of reaction out of you about it."

"You're not the whole town."

Logan didn't flinch at the bite in his tone. "No, but I am the guy who's watched you be a wingman for the last five years without you ever wanting the same in return."

"I went to school with nearly everyone of datable age in town."

"We don't always stay in town. That hasn't changed your MO."

"You know the kind of hours I work. I'm not in a position to start a prospective relationship with anyone who doesn't live here."

"Doesn't always have to be a relationship."

"Does for me." He'd tried meaningless sex. The physical

release hadn't given him what he was looking for. Not when he knew the difference of being with someone who truly mattered.

Logan tipped back his beer, nodded. "So, she's ruined you for all women."

"Don't be ridiculous," Xander snapped.

"You haven't had a serious relationship since her. Least, not one anybody knows about—which, given the grapevine in this town, I figure is probably the absolute truth."

"There have been others since Kennedy." A couple. But no one who'd really stuck.

Trish, who'd returned with their appetizers, went brows up. "How'd I not know about that?"

"It's called discretion. Go away, Trish." There was no reason for her or anybody else to know that those others had been in college, his only stint of time away from Eden's Ridge.

Logan immediately forked up some of the fries, chewing until Trish walked away to check her other tables. "I think it's that you never got any closure."

Xander tossed down his fork. "What the hell, man? You're a farmer, not Dr. Phil."

"You can take the therapist out of the master's program..."

"Which you walked away from," Xander reminded him.

"I'm just sayin'. She walked away, leaving you with the gaping question of 'Why?' I know you. That why has been driving you batshit for years. And there's probably a part of you still wondering if it's something you did or didn't do. Something that you need to learn before you can successfully be in another relationship. That makes her a mystery, and you, my fine fellow, cannot resist a mystery."

"And you can't resist an opportunity for analysis. Even though you suck at it." Scowling, Xander stabbed at the giant fried onion. Logan wasn't wrong. But damned if he was going to admit it. "Are you done playing armchair psychologist? Because I really just want to watch the game."

"Fine, fine." Logan lifted his hands in surrender. "So Tennessee's looking good in this bracket."

They talked basketball and work. Logan bitched about the tractor he had torn apart right now and how he wasn't going to get spring planting done in time if he didn't bend the bastard to his will. They made plans for poker night with some other friends next week. Degree by degree, Xander began to relax. And as he did, the single detail he'd been trying to block out all day began to circle in his mind.

Kennedy claimed to be staying in Eden's Ridge. After ten years of globetrotting, seeing and doing God knew what, she was coming home. But how long would that last? Was this just until she and her sisters sorted things with Ari and their inheritance? Would she be gone again as soon as the family situation was stable, or was she truly back in the Ridge to stay? After a decade of broader world experiences, could she possibly be satisfied by a life here?

And why the hell was he even thinking about all this? What Kennedy Reynolds did with her life was none of his concern. The only salient point in all of this was that she'd be around long enough for him to make his apology, ask his questions, and get his answers, whatever the hell they were. He'd solve the mystery and finally, at long last, move on with his life.

So why didn't that feel like enough anymore?

CHAPTER 5

"ARI'S FINALLY OUT, I think," Kennedy reported. "Poor thing is exhausted."

From her spot curled up on the sofa, Pru knit her hands. "I still wish she'd eat more than three bites at a time." She looked up as Maggie squeezed her shoulder.

"She'll get there. Everybody grieves differently." Maggie took a seat. "But now that she is effectively out of earshot for a bit, we do need to talk about what we're going to do about her."

Kennedy dropped into a chair. "Even if Mae finds her parents, she doesn't want to go back to them. They left her. There's no evidence they wouldn't do it again."

"I think we can all agree that it's best for Ari if she's kept as stable as possible. But the fact is, with Mom gone, there's no other option for her in the Ridge. The nearest placement would be in Johnson City."

"We're not shipping her off to Johnson City," Athena snarled.

"None of us wants to do that. But let's look at reality. My life is in LA. Yours is in Chicago. That leaves Pru, and as capable as she is, I don't know that she's ready to take on a daughter." Maggie shifted her gaze. "Are you?"

Before Pru could answer, Kennedy interrupted. "Excuse me, it doesn't leave just Pru. I'm here."

Athena sneered. "Oh, excuse us for not automatically assuming you were going to be a contributing member of this family."

Kennedy absorbed the lash of anger, clenching her jaw to keep from fighting back in kind.

"Athena, that's enough." Maggie's warning tone did nothing to dim the hostility radiating through the room.

"No." Kennedy straightened. "You know what, it's fine. This is good. Obviously there are things you all want—probably need—to say to me about this. Maybe it's better to say them and clear the air."

Pru looked from one sister to the next, worry etched on her pretty face. "I don't think that's such a good idea."

"I'd rather have it all laid out at once than put up with this sniping. So go ahead, Athena. You need to vent your spleen about whatever you've been carrying around. Do it. No holds barred."

Her sister's hands curled to fists, a muscle in her jaw ticking as she stared Kennedy down with gray eyes, cold as steel. "You left us," she bit out.

Expecting the accusation didn't make it sting any less. She knew well enough what she'd done. Who she'd done it to.

"You left Maggie in the middle of the biggest upheaval of her life."

Maggie wrapped both arms around her middle in an uncharacteristic show of vulnerability. "Athena, stop it. I don't want to drag this up again."

But Pandora's box had been opened. Kennedy couldn't not address it. "I didn't know you were pregnant when I left." But looking back, she'd known something was going on with her sister. The mood swings. The change in appetite. It had been her intention to sit down with Maggie after graduation and get to the bottom of it. Then her life had hit a land mine.

"Right. Of course you didn't." Athena nodded. "Because we couldn't even *find* you for two months to tell you about the baby. Never mind we were all worried sick about you. And when you did find out, you couldn't be bothered to come home."

"I didn't have the money to come home." It was a weak defense, but it was all Kennedy had. By that time, she'd made it to the West Coast, and her waitress's wages and tips were barely enough to keep a temporary roof over her head. There'd been no money for a bus ticket, and even if there had, she'd been too afraid of what would happen if she violated the terms she'd agreed to.

"Because you were too busy living your self-indulgent, grand adventure. Alone. And what the fuck was that about, leaving Xander behind? Do you know what that did to him?"

"We're not talking about Xander," Kennedy snapped. She could only cope with so much of this at once. "I did everything I could to support Maggie from where I was."

Across the room, Maggie's cheeks went white. "Do you really think phone calls and emails made up for anything? I needed you, Kennedy. If you'd really wanted to, you could've found a way home, the same way you found a way to leave."

They had no idea how much she'd wanted to come home, how much she'd wanted to be there through all of it. Especially after Maggie lost the baby. But nothing Kennedy could do would remove the axe hovering over the back of her neck. Part of the deal she'd made was never telling anyone the secret of why she'd left. Her sisters didn't even know there *was* a danger to her coming back. If she'd come home sooner, the whole house of cards would've fallen, and the family wouldn't have recovered.

Throat thick with all the things she couldn't say, Kennedy rose from her chair. "I swear to you, I'd have been here if I could."

"Oh bullshit," Athena snarled. "You made a choice. You chose yourself."

"Athena!" Pru's censure did nothing but pull their sister's glare to her.

"What? It's true."

Kennedy swallowed. "Is that really how all of you feel?"

Pru's brown eyes were full of hurt and worry. She pressed her lips together.

"Go ahead," Kennedy told her.

"I…It took Mom *dying* to get you home."

Guilt spurted through her—that she'd never come clean to her mother, never explained. That Joan had died thinking—well, Kennedy had no idea what Joan had truly thought about her leaving. She hoped like hell Mom hadn't thought it was because of her. And now it was too late. No second chances. She'd learned that those didn't exist. And that was a fact Kennedy would have to live with for the rest of her life.

Shaking with the effort of holding in a scream, she struggled to keep her voice level. "There is no answer or reason I can give you that can make up for my not being here. And I'm sorry. More than you can possibly know. But I'm asking you, for Ari's sake, to try to get past it. I'm not a kid anymore, and I'm here to help with whatever's needed."

"And we appreciate it." Pru's instant show of support helped… a little.

Maggie ran a hand through her hair. "The thing is, you've been…drifting for a decade. You've got no ambition, no training, no career. I know your heart's in the right place, wanting to help with things here, but I'm worried that you're going to end up being more a hindrance than a help."

Never mind that she didn't have an ounce of debt, and she'd successfully lived all over the world on her own merits for a decade. Because she had no home base, few worldly goods, and— thanks to the hurried trip home—almost nothing in savings, of course they'd think she'd be another burden to the family.

Because she was the screw up. She always had been. All these years she'd been on her own, she'd managed to move past that, but only a few days home, and she was being shoved back into that box.

That her sisters could so fully believe this cut deep enough to steal her breath. They didn't know her at all. Not anymore. Opening this door had been a mistake. Maybe staying was a mistake, too. They weren't going to forgive her.

Feeling trapped inside the cage of her own rage, Kennedy could hardly breathe. She needed space. She needed to move, to get the hell out of here, away from the accusatory stares before she simply exploded.

She was already halfway across the room before Athena called out after her. "Where the hell are you going?"

Kennedy stopped and turned back. "Why does it matter? As y'all have so blatantly pointed out, I have nothing—no money, no skills, no ambition. I have nothing to contribute to this family but being another burden. So why the hell should you care where I go?"

"Kennedy, please don't leave." God, she hated that Pru felt like she had to beg.

"I promised you I'd stay and see this thing through. I'm not going to break that promise, no matter what you all think of me. But right this second, I need some goddamned space."

On that she headed for the kitchen. At the back door, she didn't hesitate, didn't stop to grab a jacket or a flashlight. Even as she knew she was proving their point, the moment her feet hit the grass, she began to run.

∽

XANDER SHOULD'VE GONE home after his beer at Elvira's. It had been a long-ass week and, he should've hit the hay early, tried to catch up on some sleep. He should not have driven out to this spot to indulge in some toxic game of "What if?" Except how could he not, with everybody and their brother asking him about Kennedy?

Xander picked his way down the trail from his old Bronco. If he was going to think about her, he might as well do it in their spot. Where they'd first become true friends and, later, lovers.

Back then, they'd been trespassing. Now, he owned the land that looked out on the valley. That had been some kind of twisted decision, to buy the place when old man Miller died. He'd tried to tell himself it was just practical. The house met his needs, fit in his budget, and the view couldn't be beat. But what did he need with all that acreage of forested mountain? Except as an insulation to his self-imposed solitude, and so he could come here, from time to time, and give in to his self-indulgent memory of the girl he couldn't forget.

He'd always accepted that they were different. Hell, that had been part of the appeal. Kennedy wasn't like anyone else he knew. He'd loved her free spirit, her sense of adventure. She'd always wanted to get out and see the world, and when she'd suggested he defer college for a year to actually do it, he'd jumped at the chance. Anything to spend more time with her. They'd spent hours talking about where they'd go, what they wanted to see and do.

It had been a great dream, one he'd fully intended to execute once they had a legitimate plan, a safety net. She hadn't liked the idea of waiting on that, but she'd agreed. They'd balanced each other—her big dreaming, his practicality. He thought she'd seen that. But in the end, she hadn't been able to bend. Hadn't been able to wait. She'd walked away from him. Run, actually, in the middle of the damned night. Because he'd fucked it up, and she hadn't seen fit to give him a second chance. Straight to heartbreak. Do not pass go. Do not collect two hundred dollars.

She'd seen the world, exactly as she'd wanted, and he'd stayed here. Adventures without her hadn't held any appeal. And that had been mostly okay, once he'd accepted she wasn't coming back. He loved Eden's Ridge, loved the Smoky Mountains. He'd gotten used to his life, to the shape of it, without her. Until tragedy had suddenly thrown Kennedy back into his path.

She'd said she was staying. Did she mean it? After what she'd done, could he trust anything she said? Did it even matter?

Given how his traitorous heart had lurched at the possibility, yeah, it mattered. If she was really staying, then he had to find a way to live with her here.

A sound had Xander hesitating on the trail, something that didn't belong amid the quiet rustle of the wind and the calls of the night hunting animals. His finger hovered over the snap on his holster as he listened. Someone was…crying. And he knew. He knew even before he made it to the bottom of the trail, before he saw the slim figure standing at the edge of the overlook, her hair silvered in moonlight.

"Kennedy."

With a tiny shriek, she whirled, stumbling in the dark.

Shit! Xander leapt forward and grabbed her before she could topple over. He yanked her back, wrapping his arms around her and spinning to put himself between her and the sixty foot drop. His heart thundered at the near fall.

"Xander?" she squeaked. Her hands were fisted in his jacket. "What the hell are you doing here?

"Having a minor heart attack. You okay?" Now that the danger was past, he couldn't seem to make himself release her.

"Well, I'm not dead. How did you know I was here?"

"I didn't."

"Then what are you doing here?"

Remembering how good you feel. He was taller and broader than he'd been at eighteen. The body pressed up against his had filled out with subtle curves she hadn't had back then. But they still fit. And that was foolishness.

When he didn't answer, she asked, "Did Pru call you?"

"No." He didn't believe in lying. "I came because I was thinking about you." Even in the dim light, Xander could see the tracks of tears. He had no right to touch her, but he couldn't stop himself from cupping her face and brushing a thumb gently across her cheek. "You've been crying."

Kennedy broke away from him then. The familiar ache settled in his chest as she stepped out of his arms.

"Been doing a lot of that lately." The flippant tone didn't hide the pain beneath her words.

He'd never been able to walk away from her pain. Everything in him itched pull her in and shield her, to soothe the hurts. Once, she'd have let him. But this wasn't his Kennedy. This woman seemed far more like the skittish, mistrustful girl he'd met years ago, after she'd first come to Joan. That was its own kind of punch in the gut. Did she trust him so little now?

"What happened with your sisters?"

She wrapped her arms around her middle. "A fight that's been a long time coming. I gave them free rein to say whatever they needed to say to me, about how I left and how I've lived my life for the past ten years. I don't have a right to get upset that they took me at my word." Turning back to him, she straightened her shoulders. "And you're here, so you might as well get in your licks, too."

As if he was really going to stand here and berate her when she was already hurting? "You want me to kick some puppies, too, while I'm at it?"

"That's more consideration than I deserve. Between you and Maggie, it's a close race as to who has the most reason to hate me. But I was betting on you."

So she hadn't been off all these years thinking she was a hundred percent in the right. It was a thin opening, but one his idiot heart grabbed onto with both hands. "We all felt a lot of things when you left. But I don't think hate was really in the mix." He'd tried for a while, but it hadn't stuck.

"Not so sure you're right about that." Turning away from him, she stared out over the valley, dark now but for a few pinpoints of light from the street lamps on Main Street that never turned off and a handful of security lights here and there. "What was it like for her? Maggie."

He didn't have to ask what she meant. Perfect, over-achiever Maggie Reynolds had wound up pregnant at seventeen. The scandal had rocked Eden's Ridge. And despite her career successes as an adult, there were still people who talked about her as *that poor girl who got knocked up in high school*. He didn't doubt that subject had come up with her sisters tonight.

"What do you think? It's a small, conservative Southern town. She was ostracized, gossiped about. It didn't help matters when she wouldn't name the father."

She drew in an unsteady breath. "And after she miscarried?"

He didn't sugarcoat it. "She'd lost most of her friends. Athena was in fights every other week over the things people said. I missed a lot of it because I was off to school at UT, but it was pretty hellish. She needed her family."

Kennedy closed her eyes and a few more tears leaked out. "I couldn't come back."

And that was on him. It was long past time for him to apologize. "You've never told them why. Your sisters."

She went rigid. "Excuse me?"

"You've never told them about the fight. About what an ass I was that night."

As fuzzy as the events leading up to it were, Xander still clearly remembered being naked with her in the back of her car and not finding the condoms he'd stowed in the glove box. Cliff Newell had been messing around in there earlier that night and had taken them all. The ass. Xander had put forth all of his inebriated charm to convince her he'd pull out. Kennedy had laughed and reached for her shirt. And Xander hadn't been able to drop it.

No really. How do you not trust me?

She'd tried to put him off, but he'd just kept pushing until she'd snapped.

Excuse me for not being willing to throw away both our futures because you want to get off.

He'd been drunk and horny and so very stupid. *If you loved me, you'd trust me.*

Never in their entire relationship had he put conditions on her. For someone like her, who'd been in a string of foster homes before she came to Joan, where love and acceptance were withheld for all kinds of reasons, that was a special brand of cruelty. He hadn't thought of that in the moment, but he'd thought of it plenty since.

The adult Kennedy was staring at him, fresh tears still streaking her face. Xander felt his gut twist, remembering the same look on her face from that awful night. *If you loved me, you wouldn't ask me to take the chance.*

If you loved me. Like, for the first time, she hadn't been down-to-the-bone certain that he'd walk through fire for her. She'd certainly run away for less from many of those previous foster placements.

"I should never have pressured you. Ever. Being drunk was no excuse. And God knows, you were right. What happened to Maggie—that could have been us." When Porter had told him about Maggie's pregnancy, that fact had eaten at him.

"I can't tell you how sorry I am, how much I hated myself for the things I said. I was on your doorstep as soon as I woke up the next day, ready to grovel—hangover and all. But you were gone." And his entire world had been knocked off its axis as he'd realized that what had felt like a stupid fight to him had been so much more for her.

Xander took a step forward, starting to reach for her, to fold her into his arms, but everything in her posture shouted *hands off*. He curled his hands in on themselves. "Was it really so bad that you had to run away from me? From your family? Didn't you know me better than that?"

CHAPTER 6

*K*ENNEDY'S HEART BEAT SO hard and fast, she wondered she didn't just bleed out from the pain of seeing him look at her with all that guilt and shame. She'd been prepared for him to hate her. Ready for him to rail and rant and curse her for slinking off in the middle of the night without a word. She deserved all of that and more. But he thought he was why she'd left. All these years, he'd thought it was because of that stupid fight. She'd barely even remembered it. Why would she, given what came after? But clearly he remembered, and he blamed himself.

The absolute wrongness of that had her stepping into him before she could think better of it, laying a hand over his heart. "Xander, I—" But what could she say to allay his fears? She couldn't tell him the truth, and she didn't want to lie. Another round of tears welled up as she realized all the other ways she'd hurt him besides just walking away. "I'm so sorry."

His hand covered hers, pinning it in place. "I get why you ran. But why stay away all this time?"

It was hard to force words past the knot in her throat. "I was afraid."

"Of me?" His stunned expression sucker punched her right in the gut.

"No! Never that. I—" Kennedy took a breath, struggling to sort out what scraps of truth she could give him. "I thought you'd hate me. You had every right. I handled things so badly. I hurt everybody with how I left, and I've been afraid to come back and face that. The longer I stayed away, the worse it got, until it became this huge, overwhelming thing I didn't know how to get past. I didn't feel worthy—of the family, of forgiveness. Everybody moved on with their lives, without me in them, and I had no idea how to come back from that. And…I was terrified to come home and see you with someone else." She swallowed, wishing she hadn't let that slip out. But once the words started coming, she couldn't seem to stop them. "It's not fair or reasonable. I'm the one who walked away. I don't get the right to be upset with you for moving on with your life. But I just—I couldn't be here to see it and remember what I threw away."

Her fingers curled into the front of his shirt, as if by grabbing on now, she could somehow make up for all the years of distance, all the years of pain. A part of her wanted to keep going, to haul him into her and take his mouth, stripping the layers of clothes off that big, built body of his until they gave each other the gift of oblivion. She so desperately wanted that comfort and closeness with him. No one had ever made her feel like he did. But it wouldn't happen. After everything else she'd done, she'd never use him like that.

Before she could release him, Xander's hand slid around to cup her nape, tipping her face so she had to look at him. "There's no one else. There's never been anyone else who mattered."

Was he…Did he mean he'd *waited* for her?

The instant blast of yearning almost dropped Kennedy to her knees. To fall into his arms, into his bed, and shout yes to a question she wasn't even sure he was asking. She'd never even let herself imagine the possibility of picking back up where they'd left off, of getting the chance to build the life they'd so often dreamed of. She imagined it now, and her heart squeezed to aching. Because she knew what she could have with this man—if she had someone else's life. But she was stuck with her own life, with all its many mistakes, and they meant she couldn't have him now any more than she could a decade ago.

On the heels of that bitter thought, she was struck by a wave of fresh guilt. His life had been on hold—at least to some extent—because of her. Whether he'd been deliberately waiting for her or because he needed some kind of resolution, he'd lost ten years he could've been building his life with someone else. She didn't want that. The idea if it made her physically ill. But he deserved the chance for that, without her screwing it up.

"You're shaking." Xander's gaze skimmed over her. "Where's your coat?"

She wasn't cold. Not when her skin felt almost electrified where he touched her. "Left without it."

"You must be freezing." He slid his own coat off and swung it around her shoulders.

Kennedy barely resisted the urge to turn her face into the shoulder to inhale his scent as she slid her arms into the sleeves. Since they fell well past her wrists, Xander reached out himself and zipped her in. The fabric was still warm from his body, and she hugged it close, wishing it were him wrapping her up tight.

"C'mon. I'll take you home."

"I don't want to go home." Not that she knew what the alternatives were, but she simply couldn't face another round with her sisters tonight. Not when she felt as if she'd been flayed alive.

"Okay." The simple, easy acceptance relaxed her a fraction, enough that when he nudged her toward the trail, she fell into motion beside him. It never even occurred to Kennedy to fight it, his hold felt so right. Dangerous thinking. No matter what she wanted, she couldn't let him believe they could start this up again.

At the top of the trail, she stopped and gaped at his Bronco. "I can't believe you still have this thing."

"Why on Earth would I get rid of a solid piece of American-made steel?"

"Because it's older than we are, and you've probably paid for an entirely new car in parts by now?"

"Nah." Xander tapped the hood with affection. "Me and Jethro have been through too much to split up now."

Kennedy had spent many happy days with Xander, roaming Stone County in this thing. And quite a few nights steaming up the windows. It was impossible not to think of that as he popped the back hatch. Nerves jittered in her stomach at the idea of crawling back there with him again. Mostly because, despite her good intentions, she wasn't sure she could say no, and that was a bad, bad idea.

But after a couple of moments of digging, he came up with a quilt and shut the lift gate again. Circling around to the front, he opened the door and gestured her in. "It'll be warmer out of the wind."

Without a word, she clambered onto the bench seat ahead of him. He climbed in behind her and shut the door.

"Not much warmer in here," she said, realizing she *was* cold now that he wasn't touching her.

"It will be. Come here." Xander hauled her across the seat until her back was pressed to his chest, then flipped the blanket over them both.

It was an old, familiar gesture, one she should've resisted, for both their sakes. But she was so, so tired of being alone. If this was the only comfort she'd get, she would take it and be grateful. Relaxing against him, Kennedy willed herself not to give in to the urge to turn her face and rub it against his chest like a cat.

Xander's arms slid around her waist, as they had a hundred times before. How long had it been since someone had held her? Other than Flynn, had she trusted anyone enough for this? Just this simple touch. With a long sigh, Kennedy lay her head back against Xander's shoulder, feeling more content than she had any right to. But here was what she'd needed since her mother's death. What she'd needed for more years than she cared to admit. More than being home, more than being with her sisters, Xander had always been her safe place.

"Better?"

"Yeah." She wrapped her arms over his and let herself have the illusion that this wasn't just for tonight.

"Tell me about your travels. How did you manage it without having savings built up?" The warmth of his breath stirred her hair.

"Do you really want to hear about this? About what I've done since I left here?"

"After you left, I haunted the house, constantly stopping by, helping out. At first it was because I thought you'd turn up, and I wanted to be there when that happened. Then it was just hoping to catch any scrap of news about where you were or what you were doing. So yeah, I want to hear."

God, that hurt her heart to think about. But she did as he asked because it seemed a safer topic than some of the alternatives. "I took about a million odd jobs. Seasonal work. Trail guide. Tour guide. Ski instructor. House-sitted quite a bit professionally, so I didn't have to pay for lodging a lot of the time."

"That's a thing?"

"It is. I also bartended a lot. Waited tables. Worked as a hotel maid several times. Whatever came up. When nothing came up, I got really good at busking. Sang for my supper on more than one occasion."

"You've still got killer pipes. Joan would've liked that you sang."

Kennedy's throat went thick. "I don't want to talk about Mom," she whispered.

"Okay." He rested his cheek against her hair, and that, too, was familiar. "Then tell me where all you went."

So she did. Cuddled up in the cab of his ancient Bronco, Kennedy took him around the world to all the places she wished he could've been with her to see. She got drowsy wrapped in their little cocoon, but every time she stopped talking, he'd ask more questions. No matter how late it got, she didn't want to break the truce or spell or whatever it was that was holding the pain and grief at bay, so she answered, telling him story after story.

"Out of everywhere you've been, which place was your favorite?"

Kennedy didn't even have to think. "Ireland. It's the only country I kept going back to."

"Why's that?"

"I love it there. And I've got some good friends. I even, briefly, had a sort of music career, touring for a while."

"Really?" She could hear the smile in his voice.

"Really." She told him about Flynn and his merry band of gypsy musicians.

"So you and he...?" Xander's tone was casual. Deceptively so.

The idea that he was jealous gave Kennedy far too much satisfaction. She snorted a laugh. "Flynn Bohannon is the closest I've ever had to a brother, and that includes all of my assorted foster brothers."

"So he's family."

"He is." She sobered. "You could just ask."

"Ask what?"

"If I moved on."

"Did you?"

"I wasn't in any one place long enough to get serious with anybody." She could blame it on her mobility, but there simply hadn't been anyone who'd made her feel even a tenth of what she'd felt for Xander. What she still felt for him.

She shifted until she could look him in the face. "Xander." She didn't know what she wanted to say, what she wanted to ask. Then he cupped her face in that big, broad palm, and the words dried up, leaving nothing in their wake but a wanting she saw reflected in his eyes.

His thumb stroked her cheek, his gaze dropping to her mouth. "Kennedy."

Her breath quickened, and the air between them seemed to pulse. It was absolute madness to act on this. But had she ever used good sense when it came to Xander? She wanted him. She always had.

Her hand curled into his shirt as her heart began to thunder. The vinyl seat creaked as he shifted to lower his head.

"The sun's coming up." She blurted the words in a last ditch effort to save them both.

Xander blinked and looked out the windshield at the first sliver of daylight glimmering over the misty peaks.

The break in eye contact enabled her to regain a little control. "I should probably get home." When she pushed against his chest for leverage, he let her go, and Kennedy did her best to ignore the crushing disappointment.

As he cranked the Bronco and headed back toward her house, she told herself this was for the best. Yeah, she planned to stay in Eden's Ridge, at least so long as the family needed her. But she wasn't in any position to make promises, and she sure as hell wasn't going to do anything to yank him around again. If tonight had proved anything, it was that Xander Kincaid was a fixture in the Ridge and that wasn't going to change.

When they reached the house, he shut off the engine.

"What are you doing?"

"Well, I'm either walking you to the door or I'm helping you shimmy up the bodock tree to sneak back into your room. Your choice."

The image made her grin, which was a wholly unexpected

end to the night. There was no telling how many times she'd gone up and down that tree in the years she'd lived here. "I don't know if the window is unlocked, so I guess I'm going in the front door and hoping nobody's up yet."

They quietly climbed the steps. Kennedy checked the knob and found it unlocked. Leaving it closed, she turned back to Xander. "Thanks for last night. Being back here, dealing with Mom, with my sisters—it's been hard. You helped, more than you know."

"I'll always lend an ear. Or a shoulder. I hope you know that."

She did, and it made her feel small and unworthy, knowing she had to keep lying to him, even if only by omission. He was good man, who deserved better. Suddenly too choked up to speak, she could only nod.

"Hey. It's all right. Come here, now." Xander drew her against him, wrapping around her, until she felt surrounded, protected.

Kennedy burrowed in, holding tight and struggling not to break apart. She shouldn't do this, shouldn't lean on him. And she'd stop. In a minute. But it just felt so damned good not to be alone. To borrow someone else's strength for once.

He threaded his fingers in her hair and gently massaged her scalp. It was an old, comforting gesture, something he'd done a hundred times before that never failed to release the tension. Another few minutes, and she'd fall asleep on her feet.

"You're going to put me to sleep," she murmured.

"I can carry you up."

As appealing as that idea was, the last thing she needed was Xander anywhere near her bed. Or, worse, to run into any of her sisters, who'd assume she left last night for a booty call with her ex. Since that was definitely not happening, she needed to haul her own ass upstairs. Alone.

Intent on stepping back, Kennedy lifted her head. Whatever she'd been about to say spilled out of her head as she met his eyes. Steady and warm, they bored into hers, seeing far more than she wanted. But he'd always seen her. Hadn't that been part of his appeal?

"Xander." She didn't know if it was a warning or a plea. But she didn't move. Not when he shifted his hold from a hug to an embrace. Not when he tipped her face up to his. When his lips brushed hers, she sighed and melted into him.

He tasted like home. Like sweet tea and apple stack cake and picnics on the mountain. Like every good thing she'd denied herself for what felt like a lifetime. The slow, coaxing kiss took her back to long, lazy summer days, and—when he traced her lips with his tongue—even hotter summer nights. He swept her back to a far simpler time, when their whole lives had stretched out before them and nothing else mattered but being together.

Rising to her toes, Kennedy slid her hands into his hair, angling her mouth to take the kiss deeper as sweetness gave way to a deep, vicious need. But he didn't bow to her demand. After one quick nip, Xander eased her back from the edge, showing a ruthless patience he hadn't had at eighteen. She whimpered in protest, too far gone for sense or reason.

His voice was rough when he spoke. "Lark."

Her old nickname was another link to the past, part of a history too long denied.

"I know you've got a lot to deal with coming back. Repairing things with your sisters. Sorting things with Ari. But promise me you'll think about this, too."

With her body flushed and her lips still tingling from his, she'd have promised him anything. She managed some vague noise of assent.

Apparently satisfied with that, Xander nodded. With one last stroke of her hair, he stepped back. When she didn't move, he reached past her to open the front door and nudged her inside. "Good night," he said, and shut the door behind her.

If Xander's brain hadn't been completely scrambled, he might've remembered to get his coat back from Kennedy before he'd shoved her into the house. But it had taken every last shred of control he possessed to actually let her go instead of dragging her upstairs or to the barn or into the back of his Bronco or pretty much the nearest horizontal surface, so his coat—and the work keys in its pocket—were still with her. Which was his only excuse for showing back up at the Reynolds house an hour later, after a hurried shower and change of clothes. Well, and he already wanted to see her again.

It had felt like they were finally on the same page when he left her. But that might've been the kiss. Before she'd come back to the Ridge, he'd told himself it would be enough to apologize and be forgiven. But holding her in his arms again, knowing she was staying, just cemented what he hadn't been willing to admit to himself for years—he wanted another chance.

He was going to have be careful with her. Chemistry and old habits aside, he still needed to win back her trust. He'd given some thought to that on the way home. Kennedy was as fragile as he'd ever seen her. She'd just lost her mother, and things were an absolute mess with her sisters. He wasn't the kind of man to take advantage of that vulnerability. But he could make himself a fixture in her life again, remind her of how good they were together, and—in doing so—give her some much needed support so she didn't feel like it was just her against the world.

Xander gave fleeting thought to trying his own luck with the old bodock tree and knocking on her window like the old days. After being up all night, she'd probably gone straight to bed. But doing so under the cover of darkness was one thing. Doing it in broad daylight, when any of her sisters could look out a window or go out to the barn for something was much harder to explain. So he gave a perfunctory knock instead and hoped for the best. He fought the urge to shift from foot to foot as he sifted through excuses.

Athena tugged open the door. One brow winged up. "Can I help you, Deputy?"

"Came for coffee."

There went the other brow. "Do we look like a Starbucks?"

"Wanted to check on everybody, too."

She pursed her lips in an *I'm not buying your shit* expression but stepped back and let him inside. "There's a fresh pot on."

Xander trailed her into the kitchen.

"You're a little late. Our missing person finally turned back up."

"Your what?" At the stove, Kennedy's confused gaze shot from Athena back to him. The spatula in her hand clattered into the skillet. "Xander." Color leapt into her cheeks.

"Kennedy."

Something electric snapped between them and held. Xander shoved his hands into his pockets because he wanted to spin her around and pick right back up where they'd left off. At the table, Maggie looked from him to her sister and back, clearly trying to decide whether something needed to be said.

"Was she missing?" Xander asked.

"We weren't sure. She left in something of a hurry last night, and we didn't know if she'd come back," Maggie said.

Kennedy bristled, snatching the spatula back up. "I promised I would."

"You were upset and not thinking clearly. We were worried."

"You were worried," Athena retorted. "I just figured she'd bolt again."

A muscle jumped in Kennedy's jaw, but she said nothing, just turned back to the stove.

Pru wandered in. "I thought I saw your cruiser out there. Good morning, Xander." She slid an arm around him in an easy hug.

"Morning."

She eased back and gave him a long study. The back of his

neck prickled. It was an *I know what you've been up to* look. He knew it well enough from his own mother and hadn't thought he'd run into it here.

Athena gestured toward the counter. "You wanted coffee. There it is."

Needing to do something, he went straight to the cabinet and pulled out a mug. Kennedy was now pointedly not staring at him, focused instead on whatever it was she was messing with on the stove.

"I don't know why you're cooking. We have enough casseroles to last us for days," Athena said.

"Because I wanted something different," Kennedy retorted, sliding the skillet under the broiler.

She sounded brittle and angry. So did Athena, but that was her default state. Xander felt sure that last night's fight had originated with her. Still, tension stretched between all the sisters. He could feel it as he poured his coffee, see it in the hands Pru knotted together and the frown bowing Maggie's lips.

He laid a hand against Kennedy's lower back. "You okay?" he murmured.

She went still, curling her fingers around the edge of the counter. Because his hand was still on her, he felt the slow, controlled exhale. "Fine." The word was so low, no one else was likely to have heard.

Xander eased a little closer. "You still can't lie worth a damn."

Kennedy frowned at him. "What are you doing here?"

"My work keys are in my coat pocket."

Confusion flickered over her face for a moment before she realized what he meant. She nodded, though whether that was acceptance or some variation of *I'll take care of it*, Xander wasn't sure. She clearly didn't want to announce to the family that she'd been with him last night, so he kept his mouth shut as she nudged him out of the way and pulled the skillet back out of the oven. With careful, practiced moves, she placed a plate over the skillet and inverted it. All Xander could tell was that there were eggs involved and it smelled amazing. Maybe it was some kind of fancy oven omelet?

"What is that?"

"Tortilla Española."

He eyed the thick, steaming egg-thing. "That doesn't look like any kind of tortilla I've ever seen."

"Not that kind of tortilla. That's Mexican. This is a Spanish potato tortilla—more like a frittata—for Ari. Her grandmother emigrated from Seville, and I thought it might be something she'd have made Ari as comfort food."

"Every weekend." The quiet voice came from the doorway, and they all turned.

Ari crossed into the kitchen, her sock feet soundless on the wood floor as she came to inspect Kennedy's work. She leaned over and inhaled the fragrant steam, her dark eyes closing. "It smells like hers."

Kennedy fidgeted with a pot holder. "I thought, maybe, it might appeal more than all this other stuff."

Ari straightened and threw herself at Kennedy. Kennedy staggered back one step before she caught herself and wrapped both arms tight around the girl.

"*Gracias.*" The word came out muffled against Kennedy's shoulder.

"*De nada, hermanita.*"

Ari spilled out more rapid fire Spanish in a quiet voice, and Kennedy answered in kind. Xander had no idea what she said, except that it had the tone of promises.

Finally, stroking a hand down the girl's hair, Kennedy leaned back. "Will you eat?"

Ari nodded and reached into the cabinet for a plate. She cut herself a massive slab of the tortilla and took it to the table under the shocked gazes of the other Reynolds women. Kennedy's mouth curved in a satisfied smile.

Grabbing more plates, she looked over at him. "Well, you're here. You might as well have some breakfast."

While the rest of them filled their plates with breakfast casserole and pastries from all the food brought by the mourners—by tacit agreement, they left most of the tortilla for Ari—Kennedy excused herself. He heard footsteps on the stairs and figured she was going to retrieve his coat. From long habit, he took his breakfast to the table and sat. He'd eaten meals at this table more than a hundred times over the years. The faces had often changed, but it had always felt like a big, extended family. Now, without Joan to referee, it just felt wrong.

Maggie studied him over her coffee cup. "Xander, what are you doing?"

Being purposely obtuse, he dug into the food. "In the time-honored tradition of bachelors everywhere, I'm mooching breakfast."

"My bull—" Athena glanced at Ari. "—pucky meter is pinging,"

The teenager rolled her eyes. "I'm thirteen. I've heard swearing before."

"That's still no reason for us to use it around the table," Pru said easily.

They all looked at him expectantly. Ignoring the adults, he leaned over and aimed his fork toward Ari's tortilla.

She narrowed her eyes and brandished her knife. "Don't make me cut you."

Xander chuckled.

Kennedy came back in the room, her arms full of stuff. "Maybe let's avoid bloodshed at the dinner table. I brought down your shoes and backpack. We'll leave when you finish your breakfast." She set everything down, and Xander watched as she surreptitiously draped his coat over the seat of a barstool.

Well done, Lark.

She poured herself a cup of coffee and slid into the chair beside him.

"Aren't you going to eat?" Pru asked.

"I'll get something later."

Xander couldn't blame her. The tension in the room was probably enough to sour her stomach. In the awkward silence, he worked his way through his own breakfast and was considering seconds when Maggie rose and took her plate to the sink.

"We have a lot of work to get done today. Athena and I both need to be getting back in a few days, so whatever decisions need to be made for the short-term have to happen now."

That was obviously his cue to leave. He tried to think of something to say, some excuse to stick around. But he had his own work that he couldn't put off any longer. He slid out of his chair and laid a hand on Kennedy's shoulder, waiting until she lifted her gaze to his.

"Thanks for breakfast. If you need help with anything—whenever, wherever—just let me know."

She stared at him for a long moment before finally nodding. "Don't forget your coat."

"Right." He scooped it up from the barstool.

"You didn't have a coat when you got here," Athena put in.

Shit.

Everybody looked from him to Kennedy, who was staring at her coffee as if it held the secrets of the universe.

"Are you kidding me?" Athena asked. "She didn't do enough of a number on you ten years ago?"

Kennedy's knuckles went white around the mug, and Xander was simply done.

"You need to back off." He didn't raise his voice, but he used the same no nonsense tone he usually reserved for belligerent drunks at the tavern.

Athena wasn't cowed in the least. "Still playing white knight after everything she did." She shook her head. "Your funeral."

Xander opened his mouth to pop off, but Kennedy spoke first.

"For the love of God, both of you stop it. I'm too tired for all of this." She fixed her gaze on Athena. "I realize you're upset with me, and that's fine. It's your right. I've apologized. If you choose not to accept that, that's on you. But I'm not letting you provoke me, or anyone else, into a fight. We have too many more important things to worry about." She shoved to her feet. "Ari, it's time for us to leave for school. Xander, I'll walk you out."

Kennedy stalked out of the room and didn't stop until they hit the front porch.

Xander felt like he needed to apologize. "I'm sorry. I didn't think to get the coat back when dropped you off, and I had to have my keys."

Crossing her arms, she looked past him at the door, obviously waiting for Ari. "I don't care about that. But why are you doing this?"

"Doing what?"

She waved her hand in the general direction of the kitchen. "*That*. Whatever that was."

The lack of sleep was obviously messing with her.

"You're going to have to be more specific, Lark."

Kennedy pinched the bridge of her nose. "We aren't eighteen anymore, Xander. I'm not yours to protect. So why are you riding in here like I am?"

He didn't touch her, though he desperately wanted to. "Because you need it."

Those big green eyes went suspiciously glassy at that.

"All that—" Xander waved his own hand. "—is a damned mess. I just want you to know that you don't stand alone here."

Whatever she would've said to that got cut off by Ari bursting out of the house. Time to vacate before he mucked this up any worse. "Have a good day at school, kiddo. Kennedy, I'll see you around."

Xander gave them both a wave and headed for his cruiser.

CHAPTER 7

KENNEDY GOT BACK TO the house braced for a fight. She'd meant what she said. With everything on their plates, letting herself be provoked was a waste of precious energy and detrimental to Ari. But she didn't actually expect any of them to let it drop. Why would they? It had been open season on her since she got back Stateside, and Athena in particular seemed determined to get in every verbal jab she could —maybe because Maggie was far too controlled for something like that.

Her sisters were still in the kitchen, in the process of doing the dishes and clearing away the leftovers.

From her position at the sink Athena smirked. "Back a week and already starting things back up with the ex you left high and dry. Ballsy."

"I'm not starting anything back up with Xander. He gave me a ride. That's all."

"Clearly not the good kind. You don't look anywhere near relaxed enough for that."

Okay, that was it. Kennedy was about to drag her sister into the kind of rip-roaring, hair-pulling fight she hadn't had since she was thirteen.

"Athena, that's enough." Maggie's voice was sharp. "You've taken your potshots and now you're done. Kennedy's right. We have more important things to worry about. The status of her relationship with Xander is not one of them."

It didn't exactly qualify as support, but Kennedy would take it.

Athena scowled and plunged her hands into the soapy water.

Apparently in go mode, Maggie continued. "Now, since Athena and I only have a few days left, we need to make the most of them. There's no reason to think there's any problem keeping the house, but we should go through the whole thing, top to bottom. We're not finished with that list of items Mom bequeathed to folks, and we need to give the whole thing a good cleaning and general going over, inspecting for any problems or necessary repairs. It's a big house and it's old, so we need to be thorough and head off any issues before they turn into actual problems."

She'd made a list for each of them. Of course she had. Maggie was used to running the world, so organizing and delegating was par for the course. As soon as she'd finished giving orders, Kennedy pushed back from the table. She wanted some time alone to think and clearing out the third floor bedrooms was just the place to get it.

The third floor had originally been an attic, loosely divided into servants' quarters for the brief period when the lumber baron who'd built the place could afford them. Later generations had used it for storage, but Joan had turned them back into bedrooms when she'd exceeded the capacity of the six bedrooms on the second floor. Because there were always more children who needed a safe place to stay.

Kennedy flipped on the light in the first room. Judging by the layer of dust up here, nobody had been in residence for quite some time. Moving from room to room, she turned on lights and opened windows to let in the chilly morning air. After stripping all the beds and starting a load of linens in the washer, she hauled cleaning supplies from downstairs and began the process of dusting, scrubbing, and polishing.

The work was mindless and methodical and reminded her of her various stints working in housekeeping for various hotel chains, a couple resorts, even a B and B or two. It hadn't been her favorite job, but it had been honest work. There was something satisfying about putting things to rights and leaving a space ready for its next guest. Not that these rooms were likely to see more guests. Even if Pru opted to adopt Ari, Kennedy highly doubted she was interested in taking on Mom's mantle and rescuing all the lost children. Joan's death meant the end of an era. The thought made Kennedy ache all over again.

"I don't think anybody's been up here in a while."

At the sound of Pru's voice, Kennedy scrubbed a hand over her wet cheeks. "It seems to have escaped Mom's last deep clean."

Pru came into the room, wrapping an arm around her shoulders. "What's wrong?"

"I was just thinking how sad it is. I mean, apart from all the obvious reasons, but this is the end of the Misfit Inn."

A bittersweet smile curved Pru's lips. "I'd forgotten about that." She looked around the room. "Joan's Misfit Inn, home for the wayward."

"And sometimes wicked," Kennedy finished, mustering a smile of her own.

"She wouldn't have had it any other way."

"Can you imagine if she had? One person rattling around in this monstrous house? Who on Earth needs eleven bedrooms?"

"No sane person," Pru agreed.

"It's a good house, though. You can feel all the love that soaked into the walls." Kennedy ran a hand over the chair rail she'd just polished. "All the rooms could use more than a good cleaning. A fresh coat of paint would go a long way toward perking everything up."

"No sense in that if no one's going to be using the rooms. We should probably shut off this floor of the house to save a bit on the utility bills."

That was the practical thing, of course. But Kennedy felt more than a little disappointed. She couldn't put her finger on why. Untapped potential, she supposed.

"Look, Kennedy, I wanted to talk to you."

She stiffened at Pru's serious tone. "About?"

"Last night for starters. What's going on with you and Xander?"

"Nothing." The reply was automatic, if not exactly accurate. She didn't have a damned clue what was going on with her and Xander.

"I heard you get home this morning. That kiss didn't look like nothing."

Blood rushed to Kennedy's cheeks at the realization that moment hadn't been as private as it had felt. Of course Pru was the little mother, who wouldn't have been able to sleep without everyone home under one roof.

"He started it."

"You were fighting him off so hard."

Kennedy snorted at the wry tone. "Things are…complicated."

"You were with him last night."

"Not like *that*. I took a walk and hiked out to our old spot to think. He showed up and we spent all night talking."

"*Just* talking?" Pru looked askance at that.

"Yeah, just talking. Until he dropped me off. And that…I don't know what that was."

Yes she did. It was temptation. He was everything she'd never wanted to lose, and clearly he was opening that door again. Even thinking about it was so very dangerous. She needed to sleep and keep herself busy until her defenses were shored up again.

"Considering y'all nearly set the porch on fire, I've got a pretty good idea what that was."

"We still have chemistry."

"He still has feelings for you."

Kennedy bristled. "And is this the part where you warn me away, tell me not to play with him because he's been hurt enough? Because I'm aware of that, Pru."

Of course, even her gentle-hearted sister wasn't worried about *her* being hurt again. No one had any idea what it had done to Kennedy to leave. And why should they? She'd never told anyone the truth.

Pru just studied her with steady brown eyes. "No, this is supposed to be the part where I ask if you still have feelings, too. But I think you just answered that question. Yes, your leaving devastated him, but I think it devastated you, too."

Kennedy's gaze shot to her sister.

"Everyone else was caught up in Maggie's drama at the time, and it was easier for them to believe you were being selfish. But I know better. I know you. I *know* how much you loved him. And I know you wouldn't have left without a damned good reason. Not him and not us."

Kennedy schooled her features into what she hoped passed for a neutral expression. "I can't talk about it, Pru."

Her sister frowned. "Honey, were you pregnant?"

It was the absolute last thing she'd expected to fall out of Pru's mouth. "What?"

"You didn't let any of us even see you for a year. And with everything going on with Maggie at the time...I wondered."

Kennedy had to actually sit down on the edge of the bed as the gravity of that idea sank in. "Jesus. No. We were careful."

"So was Maggie. Careful doesn't always cut it."

"I wasn't pregnant. If I had been...God—" She loosed a breath. "I could never have kept Xander's child from him. And it wouldn't have been in me to give that child up." Because it would've been a part of him.

Pru sank down onto the bare mattress beside her. "I always wondered what would happen when you two saw each other again."

"I thought he'd hate me."

"Mom and I had money on how long it would take you two to rip each other's clothes off."

Kennedy's mouth fell open. "You did not!"

"Hand to God."

Fire burned in her cheeks. "I don't even want to think about you two discussing my sex life. I prefer to believe Mom didn't know I *had* a sex life."

"Oh please, like you were stealthy climbing up and down that bodock tree? Besides, back then the two of you threw off enough pheromones to choke a horse. Her biggest concern was that you were safe and that you loved each other."

"You're a cruel woman, Pru, taking away my delusions."

Pru laughed and gave her a squeeze. "Same concerns still apply." She sobered. "It must have been really hard for you to face him after all this time."

"It was easier than facing all of you."

Pru sighed and wrapped her in a tight hug. "I'm sorry about last night."

Kennedy jerked her shoulders in a shrug. "I invited it."

"Maybe so, but you still didn't deserve that. You're hurting as much as the rest of us."

"I've been putting that confrontation off for years. I figured ripping the Band-aid off would be the way to go because I didn't think I could possibly hurt any worse." She flashed a humorless smile. "I forgot Athena likes to go for the jugular."

"She'll come around. They both will."

"Hope springs eternal," Kennedy muttered.

And if they didn't, at least they'd both be heading back to the city soon enough.

~

HOW A DEPARTMENT the size of theirs, in a county of only twenty-thousand people, continued to generate this much paperwork, Xander would never know. But for once he was glad of the distraction. He was staying away from Kennedy for the moment, both because he couldn't think of a reasonable excuse for just popping in again and because he knew that, with Maggie and Athena leaving soon, she really would be busy. Plus, he wanted to see what she'd do. That hadn't stopped him from thinking about her the past three days, so he'd buried himself in paperwork, something he usually avoided on pain of death.

"Do you have that file on the Pearson case?"

Without looking up, Xander shoved the relevant folder to the edge of his desk. Leanne picked it up but didn't move.

"Something else you needed?" he asked, eyes firmly fixed on the ancient monitor.

The front door to the station opened.

At this point even old Mrs. Matisse, with her weekly complaint about Lettie Wardlaw's latest supposed attempt to sabotage her prize roses, would be a welcome interruption. But it wasn't old Mrs. Matisse standing awkwardly in the entryway. It was Kennedy.

The rush of pleasure was swift, and Xander had to fight the urge to leap out of his chair to greet her. He noted her stiff posture and the way her eyes darted around the bullpen, and it occurred to him maybe something was wrong. So he did rise and scoot out from behind his desk. "Hey Kennedy. Everything okay?"

"Hey. Everything's fine." More with the guilty fidgeting.

What on Earth did she have to be guilty about? Or maybe it

wasn't about guilt so much as being seen with him in public. There was no way people were going any easier on her than they had been on him, Joan's death notwithstanding. The Ridge's number one pastime was gossip, and respect for the grieving daughter would only go so far.

Her gaze landed on Leanne and lingered a moment before she gave an awkward little wave. "Hi."

"Kennedy, this is Chief Investigator Leanne Hammond. She's the new kid in town. Leanne, Kennedy Reynolds. "

Something in her face relaxed. Had she been jealous there for a second? The thought shouldn't please him so much.

Leanne rolled her eyes. "Six months isn't enough time for that label to wear off?"

"Sugar, six years probably won't be enough time for you to be considered a local with that Yankee accent." Xander gave her a significant *don't you have work to do* look.

"Yeah whatever, Kincaid. Nice to meet you, Kennedy." Leanne didn't leave, but at least she retreated to her desk on the other side of the room.

Before he could say anything else, Essie came in from the break room. "Why Kennedy Reynolds, as I live and breathe. How are you, sweetheart?"

A look of vague panic crossed Kennedy's face as she was subjected to the awkward *you're basically a stranger but this is the small town south and I knew your mama* hug. "I'm doing okay."

"I'm so sorry about your mama. She was a good woman."

"Thank you, Mrs. Vaughn."

"If there's anything I can do to help, you just let me know."

"Yes ma'am. Thank you. And I was so sorry to hear about Mr. Vaughn. He was my favorite teacher."

Essie's late husband, Henry, had been the music teacher at the high school. One of the few Kennedy had actually gotten along with. After a long fight with cancer, he'd finally passed away about three years before.

The older woman's eyes went a little glassy. "Thank you, honey. We had a good run." She squeezed Kennedy's shoulders and sniffed. "He always loved you."

Xander was shocked Essie didn't give her the third degree—where all she'd been, what she'd been doing— but then the older woman only retreated so far as her desk across the room. Asking additional questions was hardly necessary when she could just eavesdrop. She wasn't even subtle about it, sitting there with her hands clasped over her heart as she watched. Maybe he should offer to make some popcorn.

Because he wanted to reach for Kennedy, Xander shoved his hands in his pockets. "Was there something we could do for you?"

She finally stopped looking at everything else in the room and met his gaze. "I need you."

Her words shot straight down his spine and into his dick, which was more than ready to comply.

Two bright flags of color bloomed in her cheeks. "Your back, I mean. And maybe a friend's if you can round someone up."

That definitely took a different turn than he'd expected. "Sorry?"

"You said you were happy to help with whatever, wherever. Pru's moving into the big house until further notice, and I—We were hoping you could help us out."

"Oh."

She shoved her hands into the back pockets of her jeans and hunched her shoulders. "I'd have called, but I don't actually have a phone. I mean, an American phone. Yet. It's on the list."

Kennedy was nervous. He hadn't seen her babble this badly since the entire eighth grade class was forced to audition for the middle school play. Was she nervous to be around him, or was there something about being in the Sheriff's Office?

"Anyway, I had to run by the pharmacy to pick up some stuff, and I thought I'd take a chance you'd be here and just stopped by."

Once he was reasonably sure she'd run out of steam, he offered what he hoped was a reassuring smile. "Of course. I'm happy to help. I've got a buddy or two I can tap for extra manpower. Trucks too, if needed."

"It's not the whole house, just a few key pieces. Mostly for the business. She's still got her portable massage table, but since there's plenty of space at Mom's house, she's going to turn one of the downstairs rooms into her work space for now."

"Makes sense. I never did think it was a great idea for her to travel to clients."

They lapsed into silence. Big green eyes watched him, as if, now that she was looking, she couldn't drink in the sight of him fast enough. Xander could relate. He was starved for her touch, the taste of her. Never in his entire career as a cop had Xander cared that he didn't have an office. He preferred being out patrolling, doing his job. But damn, what he'd give for a private space with a door right now.

"Are Maggie and Athena still here?"

"For the moment. Athena goes back to Chicago tomorrow. Maggie's trying to take a few more days to line some things up. We've been doing a huge clean of the house."

That explained the faint scent of lemon oil and the little smudge of dirt on her cheek.

"You've got a little something—" Xander started to just point but couldn't help himself. He reached out to brush a thumb over the smudge.

Kennedy's long lashes fluttered closed and she turned into his touch, some of the tension melting out of her.

A door behind him opened. Kennedy looked over his shoulder and snapped ramrod straight, stepping back. Xander dropped his hand.

"Kennedy." There was nothing overtly hostile about his father's tone, but if he and Kennedy had been a couple of cats, they'd have been hissing at each other, hair standing on end.

"Sheriff."

"My condolences about your mama."

"Thank you, sir. It's hit us all pretty hard."

"I'm sure it has." Buck nodded for emphasis. "A big disruption to all of you, too. Though I guess it's time you're all getting back to your lives, now the funeral's past."

What the hell? He was practically shoving her out of town. Xander knew his father didn't like Kennedy, but he never would've guessed Buck would be outright rude. Especially in the wake of Joan's death.

A muscle jumped in Kennedy's jaw. "Maggie and Athena will be leaving this week. I'm staying to help Pru."

"Are you now?"

"It's what you do for family." Kennedy all but bit the words out. Turning to Xander, she said, "I need to be getting home." She was already backing toward the door.

Xander sure as hell didn't blame her. "Let me make some calls. I'm sure I can round somebody up by the end of the day."

"We appreciate it. Just come on by Mom's whenever. We'll owe you."

"Sure. See you later."

A quick jerk of her head served as a goodbye, and then she was gone. If she'd left any quicker, he'd have expected plumes of smoke in her wake.

Buck was already striding back to his office.

Temper simmering, Xander followed, shutting the door behind him. "What the hell was that?"

Behind his desk, Buck fixed him with a gimlet stare. "Son, don't get involved with that girl again."

Xander had had enough. "First, she's not a girl, she's a woman. Second, who I'm interested in is none of your goddamned business."

"Don't be so damned prickly. I'm just looking out for you. I'm telling you, she'll leave at the first opportunity."

"She's staying. She's made a promise to her family, and she's going to see that through."

"Seems to me, once upon a time, she made a promise to you. We see how well she kept that."

Even knowing her reasons, that blow still stung, as Buck had meant it to. His father didn't know about the fight or the role Xander had played in driving Kennedy away.

"We're not kids anymore, Dad. I'm not going to judge her now for something she did when she was just eighteen. And whatever happens with Kennedy, I'm going to support her and Pru and the rest of the Reynolds family however I can because Mom, at least, raised me better."

He stalked out of his father's office and went to call Logan about a truck.

CHAPTER 8

"I DON'T KNOW ABOUT this." Pru bit her lip as they all scanned Joan's sitting room.

"With the half-bath, this room makes the most sense," Maggie said practically. "Clients can undress or dress in there and feel a bit more private than they might anywhere else. Plus, it's got a door and can be closed off from the rest of the house if something else were going on. It's quiet. That was the whole reason Mom picked it."

"But it was Mom's space," Pru said. "To do this, we have to move all her stuff, and that just feels...wrong. Too soon."

Kennedy wrapped an arm around her. "We're not getting rid of anything. We're just rearranging. You agreed that having a room for your massage clients to come here makes the most sense for now."

"I know, but..."

"And the guys are going to be here soon to help move furniture, so we need to clear things out as best we can. Plus, I have a plane to catch, so this is literally the last thing I can help with before I go," Athena added. "Chop chop."

Pru sighed. "All right. We'll shift things to Mom's room for now."

They all pitched in, packing up the books, the knitting supplies, the prodigious supply of yarns, and all the other detritus that made up their mother's personal space. Often with so many children in the house, she'd needed a room to get away from all the noise and chaos. This one, at the back of the house, looking out over the mountains, had been her retreat. Kennedy remembered many long conversations, where she'd curled up on the floor at Joan's feet helping to ball yarn. Pru stared at that same spot on the floor, her hands hesitating over the contents of the little writing desk, while Athena and Maggie carried the ottoman out of the room.

"I don't know how my clients are going to take to this. They're used to me coming to them."

Determined to be positive, Kennedy continued to load the contents of the bookcase into boxes. "It's a good room for relaxing. That's what your clients ultimately want, right?"

"Of course. But I don't know how well they'll relax if I can't. I don't know if I can work in here."

"Is it that everything in here reminds you of Mom?"

"Doesn't it you?"

"Sure. I will forever see her sitting in that chair with her knitting needles. But she'd want the space to be used. You know she wasn't the kind of woman who was into having a shrine."

"I know. I just...this is hard."

"We need to make you think of something else when you come in here," Kennedy declared.

"How?"

"We'll make it look different. Once we carry out the furniture that's in here, we can have the guys haul in that cabinet from upstairs. You can use it for towels and supplies. We'll put up some gauzy curtains, set up a little sound system so you can play relaxing music. Maybe get one of those little water feature things.

How much better might people be able to relax if they aren't looking through the hole in your massage table to see that one random toy they didn't get kicked out of the way before you showed up. We should really play up the idea of a sort of mini-spa."

Athena came in on the tail end of that. "A spa? Really? Because anybody would come to Eden's Ridge for that? Maybe we'd like to hook it on to the Snort and Curl and make a real high class establishment."

Kennedy glared. "Don't be a snob."

"Not a snob. A realist." She plucked up another huge basket of yarn. "I've been to high class spas. Nothing about the Ridge is high class."

Kennedy bit back whatever retort she might have made. This was about making things easier on Pru and Athena wasn't helping. "Whether you're in the French Alps or in Tennessee, massage is a luxury."

"My kind of massage is physical therapy," Pru said.

"It can be both. Athena's right that we aren't crazy and high class. We're not trying to be. That doesn't mean you can't still give clients an experience that takes them temporarily out of their lives, out of their worries for a little while."

"I do have at least some clients who would probably be into that."

"And it's possible that kind of setup could attract some more clients."

"More business would certainly not be a bad thing."

"If you're not having to add in travel time, you would actually have more time available to book extra clients," Maggie added.

"Not to mention the savings on gas," Kennedy added.

"I'll get used to it. And having the room look different would help," Pru conceded.

Happy she seemed to have made things at least a little better for her sister, Kennedy threw herself into packing, half her mind on how they could redecorate the room. Filling one box, she reached for another. The top shelf was full of albums. As Pru came back in, she asked, "When did Mom get into scrapbooking?"

"About the time you started sending postcards home."

Curious, she opened one at random and found postcards and letters she'd sent from Prague. There were also emails and printed pictures.

"She's got your entire time abroad covered in there," Pru added.

Kennedy stared at her. "Seriously?"

Pru grabbed another volume and opened it to the front to display a map with a route highlighted. "She saved everything you ever sent and even made notes when you called, what news you shared or what you'd been doing. I think it made her feel closer to you, when you were so far away."

A lump set up in Kennedy's throat. "I...I had no idea. I mean, I know my being gone was hard on her, and I tried to keep in touch as best I could. But I never imagined..."

This time Pru was the one to wrap an arm around her shoulders. "She missed you. We all did. But she was so terribly proud of what you were doing, all the adventures you were having."

After all the flack she'd caught from her sisters about being immature, selfish, aimless, the idea that her mother had actually been proud was a bittersweet pill to swallow. Her eyes burned with a fresh round of tears.

"I wished she was with me. So I tried to paint as vivid a picture as I could so she sort of could be."

"She loved that. I did too. It was exciting to hear about what all you were doing. And she loved the trip you took her on more than you can possibly know. You gave her something there that none of the rest of us could."

Kennedy thought of her blog. She'd never told anyone in the family about it. It had been easier to share with strangers. But her mother would've loved it. And she would've been ecstatic about the idea of turning it into a book. But Kennedy had never responded to the editor, and the window for that opportunity was no doubt closed. It didn't matter. She couldn't afford to be so self-indulgent. There were other things to worry about.

They both lapsed into silence as Athena and Maggie came in for another load. When they'd walked out again, Kennedy wrapped Pru in a tight hug. "Thank you. I can't tell you what it means to me to know that. To know that she didn't hate me for going. That you didn't."

Pru squeezed her back and looked after where their sisters had disappeared. "They don't hate you either. They just don't understand. They'll come around eventually."

Maybe. But at this point, Kennedy was looking forward to both of them heading back to their own lives and having some time to actually heal.

She boxed up all the albums and carted them to her own room. Later, when she wasn't feeling quite so raw, she'd go through them. It'd be nice to see what Mom thought about where all she'd been. And it might be fun to revisit her travels. She spent most of her focus on the present or the future. Rarely the past.

The sound of the front door opening drew her to the top of the stairs. Xander stepped in, his eyes seeming to zero in unerringly on her. The quick curve of lips was so familiar, so welcome, she almost trotted straight down the stairs to lay a big, fat kiss on him, as she would have years ago. Then another man, slightly shorter, stocky, with a close cropped beard, came in behind him and saved her from herself. Whatever was happening between her and Xander, letting themselves fall back into old habits and pretending the past decade hadn't happened would be a mistake.

"Thanks for coming," she told him.

"No problem. This is my buddy, Logan Maxwell." Xander

thumped him on the shoulder. "He's a farmer by trade, so he's got a good, strong back."

Logan looked utterly unperturbed. "I take it you're Kennedy."

"I am." She shook his hand.

"Heard a lot about you."

Kennedy's gaze flicked to Xander.

"Mostly not from him," Logan added.

"Then I'd wager only about thirty percent of it is actually true," she said.

Her sisters came into the foyer, Athena laden with bags, and Xander made introductions to Logan.

Athena actually made nice for a full ninety seconds. "I hate to hi and bye, but I've got a plane to catch."

"And I need to drive her." Maggie winced.

"Don't worry about it. We've got things covered here," Kennedy assured her.

Maggie didn't look entirely sure of that, but what was she going to say? It wasn't as if Kennedy and Pru couldn't handle the finger pointing required to get a few pieces of furniture moved.

Pru wrapped Athena in a hug. "Be safe. Call us when you land and when you get home."

Athena rolled her eyes but squeezed Pru back. "I'll call when I land, but I'm going straight to the restaurant. I'll be home super late."

"Text at least."

"Yes, ma'am." Athena pulled back and faced Kennedy. She fidgeted. "Keep the little one out of trouble, will you?"

It was a task that presupposed she was actually staying. Kennedy decided that counted as progress. She nodded. "We'll let Ari know you said goodbye."

Athena scooped up her bags, dashing any vain hope that they might make more of a connection.

"Have a good flight," Kennedy told her, and led the guys to the back of the house to show them the sitting room.

Xander cornered her in the hall, while Logan was sizing up the furniture. "You okay?"

She tried to work up a smile for him. "Getting there."

He looked at her with dark brown eyes that always saw too much. She'd never wanted to hide from that compassion before. She didn't actually want to hide from it now. She wanted to revel in it, take the comfort and closeness she knew he'd offer. Fighting those urges was getting harder every time she saw him.

"Let's get to work."

By the time they'd relocated Mom's favorite chair to Pru's room and shifted the bookcase to a different wall, Maggie and Athena were pulling out of the driveway. Without the pair of them in the house, it felt like maybe Kennedy could breathe again.

"Now comes the fun part," she declared.

"Yeah? What's that?" Xander asked.

"Treasure hunting in the hay loft."

When the attic had been converted to bedrooms, Joan had taken to storing spare furniture and other assorted junk on the second floor of the barn. It wasn't the easiest place to haul furniture in and out of, but there were, at least, stairs. Kennedy dragged a reluctant Pru out to see what they could find.

"I'd forgotten how much stuff was up here," Pru said. "There are probably some pieces we could sell." She wandered on down one of the haphazard aisles.

"Long as you don't sell this," Xander murmured.

"Sell what?" Kennedy asked.

He tugged her behind a stack of boxes and pointed down another aisle to a dusty day bed at the other end. At the sight of it, her cheeks caught on fire.

"I have particularly fond memories of rainy afternoons and that bed." His voice was a low rumble in her ear, part seduction, part amusement. He wasn't holding her, but she could feel the heat of his body bare inches from hers.

"Maybe you want to buy it for your place," she suggested, her tone coming off a lot more flip than she felt. *Careful, girl. You're playing with fire.*

"Maybe I do." Heat flashed in his eyes.

Kennedy felt an answering tug low in her belly. *Not a good idea.* But her inner voice of protest was getting weaker, lost somewhere behind the part of her that had been drooling watching him use those big muscles to heft furniture. If it had just been her, she wouldn't have acted on the heat. She wasn't the kind of woman to throw herself at a man. But the fact that he unquestionably wanted her back made it so much harder to choose the right thing.

"So I'm gonna owe you for moving all this crap. You should probably be thinking about what you want as payment."

Why was she bringing this up right now? When they both had sex on the brain?

"Oh, I already know what I want."

The thumb he rubbed down her forearm should not have been arousing. It should have been an easy, affectionate sort of gesture. But it set her on fire.

Maybe…maybe they both needed this. He needed to get her out of his system and she needed…him. She'd always needed him. Maybe this could help grant them both some resolution and clarity.

"Do you now? And what, pray tell, is that?"

"Dinner."

Not what she'd expected him to say. "What?"

"I want you to come cook me dinner. At my place."

"You want me to cook for you?"

"Well, you already proved you're a pretty damned good cook with breakfast for Ari. And I want to spend some time with you. We've got a lot of catching up to do, and I'd just as soon do it without prying eyes or ears."

Kennedy could get behind that idea. At the Sheriff's Office, she'd felt on display during their conversation. And that had been before her run-in with his father. The thought of Buck had her hesitating, her enthusiasm dimming.

"Your daddy still hates me."

"I'm not in the habit of doing what my father wants."

The last ten years would seem to contradict that, but maybe Xander was up for letting her corrupt him again. Kennedy thought she'd enjoy that a helluva lot.

"How's tonight?"

"Sounds perfect."

~

"I can't believe you bought old man Miller's place."

Xander stepped back to let Kennedy inside. "The irony is not lost on me."

She breezed past him, her arms loaded down with bags. "Worse, I can't believe we were this close to your house the other night, and we sat in your Bronco until dawn."

He trailed her into the kitchen, effectively boxing her in against the counter as she set the groceries down. He let his lips curve, his voice drop to a growl. "I don't think either of us was complaining about close quarters that night."

She pressed a hand to his chest, and he thought she might push him away. Instead, her pupils dilated and her fingers curled in the front of his shirt.

"How hungry are you?"

Xander knew they weren't talking about food. "Starved."

"Me too." She tugged his shirt and he went willingly.

Her mouth took his, warm and insistent. An answer to the question that had been humming between them for days. Apparently she'd thought about them and had finally come up with an answer. Thank God. She'd always been the answer for him. Twining her arms around his shoulders, she took them deeper, a quick, reckless slide toward madness. They weren't outside. They had no audience. And he'd wanted the possibility of this when he'd invited her over.

Running his hands down her back, he cupped her exquisite ass and pressed her against the evidence of his need. She nipped his lip before licking to soothe, then running her tongue along the seam of his mouth. He welcomed her, stroking his tongue against hers and bending until he could hook his hands behind her legs and lift her onto the island.

Something clattered. Kennedy's head jerked toward the noise, and she reached out to nab the bottle of wine before it rolled off. "We'll just put that over there, where it'll be safe." She stretched, putting it and the other bags out of harm's way before looping an arm back around his shoulders and pressing her free hand to the pulse in his throat.

Xander could feel it hammering against her touch, could see an answering flutter at the base of her throat, and knew they could lose themselves. He wanted that, wanted to feel the softness of her skin sliding against his, the warmth of her body closing around him. He wanted it like he wanted his next breath.

But he saw something in her eyes. Some trace of desperation that had nothing to do with arousal. He knew if he kissed her again, they'd finish this. But he had a sense that if they did, it would be less about him, less about them, and more about distraction. Not that he had a problem being her distraction, but he didn't think that's what she actually needed right now.

"Tell me what's wrong."

"We are both wearing entirely too many clothes."

Xander huffed out a laugh. "That is probably true. But I didn't actually invite you over here for this."

One blonde brow shot up. "After all that innuendo in the barn?"

"I didn't say I wasn't thinking about it." He glanced down at the irrefutable evidence below his belt. "But I wasn't going to push."

She hooked her fingers in his belt, looking at him through lowered lashes. "I believe all evidence indicates that I was pulling."

Her words and the proximity of her hands had Xander thinking about those slim fingers wrapped around him, as, he imagined, she'd known it would. His dick jumped, totally on board with that plan. In a bid for some kind of sainthood, he grabbed her wrists and moved her hands back to the counter. "You forget that I know you. Sex is always your favorite distraction."

"I don't recall you complaining."

No. No he hadn't.

It had been her idea to lose their virginity together at seventeen. Who was he to say no to that? He'd had a pulse, and he'd have done anything she asked. He had. It hadn't been until later that he'd found out she'd gotten word that her father had been killed in an accident, when his rig jackknifed during a thunderstorm. Their first time had been as much about losing her grief for a while as it had been about them.

And now Joan had been victim of a weather-related accident as well. He should've seen the parallel sooner.

Xander laced his fingers with hers and kept his voice gentle. "Talk to me. You used to be able to."

"You were prettier than my therapist."

"Kennedy."

She sighed, irritation quickly being chased by resignation across her face. "Fine. I might as well start supper. I need something to do with my hands."

He had another quick mental flash of those hands on him, but he stepped back as she slid off the counter. She turned her back to him, shoulders stiff, and reached for the bags of groceries. For one last moment, he crowded in behind her, sweeping her hair to the side, so he could press a kiss to her nape. She stilled, hands fisted in plastic sacks, as if absorbing the connection. She'd said there'd been no one serious. He wondered if there'd been anyone at all. She seemed as starved for affection now as when she'd first come to Joan.

"What can I do to help?" he asked.

She tugged a bag over. "Peel these carrots and scrub up the potatoes."

Okay, not exactly what he'd meant, but he could work with that. He took the bag. "Tell me how you're really doing being back. I know it can't be easy."

The corner of her mouth quirked. "Not even a little emotional foreplay?"

"You were always more a rip the Band-aid off type. You'll feel better when you talk about it."

"It should be annoying that you still know me so well." She pulled a pair of fat pork chops from another bag. "No, it's not easy. Though I daresay the Ridge in general is more accepting of my being back than my sisters, if for no other reason than I'm a new and interesting topic of gossip."

"I've gotten my fair share of that since you got back."

"Have a cast iron skillet?" she asked.

Xander pulled one out of the drawer, and she set the oven to preheat.

"Things are rough with your sisters. You'd mentioned a fight the other night."

"We're all messed up in our own ways. Adding all our grief over Mom has made things kind of ugly. They were already angry with me, and that's been bleeding over."

"Bleeding over how?"

"Pot shots from Athena. Which is entirely to be expected. She's always had anger issues, and she'll take them out on the nearest target. I think she may be angrier with me for not coming home when Maggie got pregnant than Maggie herself. Or, I don't know. Maggie was…is pissed, too, but it's not her way to let it all hang out there. She represses every damn thing and tries to control every last detail. It's just been…shitty. To Athena, I haven't been a participating member of this family in a decade, so I really shouldn't have a say in anything going forward. I don't have the right or the basis to say what Mom would've wanted. With the house. With Ari."

"That's ridiculous. It's not like you were excommunicated."

"I think Athena feels like I excommunicated myself. And I sort of did. Not that I think that gives her license to take shots at me. But I know her. It's part of her grieving process, so I'm not fighting back." Which was a far cry from the all out wars they'd sometimes fought as teenagers. Athena had usually won those battles. He'd often been the one to deal with the aftermath.

"That's got to burn. Just sucking down whatever you're feeling about it."

She mixed together salt, pepper, garlic powder, and thyme in a small bowl, then sprinkled both sides of the pork chops with the mix. "Not half as much as Maggie's disappointment in me."

Xander frowned. "Why is she disappointed? Because you weren't here during Babygate?"

Kennedy twitched her shoulders. "That's a big part of it. And she thinks I never grew up. I've been running around the world in pursuit of my own selfish, Peter Pan dreams, while the rest of them became productive members of society."

The snap of defensive temper left him speechless for a moment. "She said that to you?"

"I'm sure, under better circumstances, she'd frame it as being upset that I'm not meeting my potential or some similar crap. But in a nutshell, due to my aimlessness and total lack of ambition, she's worried I'll just end up another burden on the family."

"How can she think you'd be a burden? You've worked. You've always worked. How else does she think you've lived all over the world?"

"Ah, but it was all temporary, short-term, low-skill and therefore low-wage kind of labor. None of which applies here. In her eyes, I have no degree, no education, no long-term job experience, and thus, very little to recommend myself to prospective employers."

"Your mother just died and you've changed your whole life to come back here. Does she seriously expect you to have it all figured out already?"

Another shoulder twitch. "It's Maggie. She would. Or she'd try. She *is* trying to sort out the state of Mom's finances with Mom's attorney." She took the carrots and potatoes from him, chopping with a chef-like efficiency before drizzling everything in olive oil and tossing with the remaining herb mixture. "But she doesn't understand that she doesn't need to sort me out, too. And I don't think any of them *really* believe that I'm here to stay."

"Have they seen you with Ari?" he demanded. "Are they blind? She's attached to you, and I saw you the other morning. You aren't going to walk away from her. That much was obvious in five minutes."

Kennedy slid the skillet into the oven and set the timer on the microwave. "She reminds me so much of me. If she sees even a glimmer that she's going to be turned over to someone else without her own wants being taken into account, she'll bolt. So, no, I'm not going to walk away from her."

"Do you think she's a flight risk?" Xander had worked his fair share of runaway cases and knew that too often they didn't turn out well.

"I would've been under these circumstances."

"Have you talked to your sisters about all this?"

"I was trying the night of the fight. But they assume that since I haven't known Ari before now, that I don't understand her and I don't have anything of value to offer on the discussion."

Xander kept hearing echoes of the same things—value, worth, merit—all things she'd struggled with since they were kids because she didn't fit the traditional mold for anything. And it infuriated him that her sisters would add to that rather than build her up.

"What about Pru?" he asked. "What has she had to say about you being back?"

Something flickered over Kennedy's face. "We had a good talk the other day. While she maybe doesn't know what I bring to the table in terms of the future, she's happy to have me home. And I admit, it's nice to have at least one person on my side."

Xander stepped into her, brushing a thumb over her cheek. "I hope you know she isn't the only one."

Kennedy angled her face into his touch, but she didn't move her gaze from his. "Why?"

Because I still love you. The certainty of it sank into his bones, and with it, a realization that she could absolutely slay him. Again. But it was her. For him, it had always been her, so he was willing to take the risk.

Xander framed her face between his palms. "Because of this."

He kissed her, not with an intent to seduce or to spread the heat that always seemed to bubble in his blood around her, but to pour out the deep well of sweetness she inspired. No one else had ever made him want to give tenderness. But she did—his beautiful, broken gypsy.

By the time he eased back, she was shaking. Her pupils were huge and her hands were curved around his forearms. Xander didn't feel entirely steady himself.

"I'm sorry," she whispered, her expression stricken. "I'm sorry I walked away from you. And I don't know if it matters to you or not, but I thought of you every day. I missed you every day."

"It matters." He wrapped his arms around her. "But I'm not worried about the yesterdays anymore. Let's just focus on the now."

CHAPTER 9

"*H*AVE A GOOD DAY at school, sweetie." Maggie hugged Ari.

The girl submitted to the embrace for a few moments before edging away with an awkward shuffle of feet. "Have a good trip back." Ari focused on the toes of her hot pink Chuck Taylors.

"I'll be back as soon as I'm able to rearrange some things at work," Maggie promised.

Another small head bob from Ari.

"Got your lunch, kiddo?" Kennedy asked. She got actual eye contact, and that felt like a victory.

"Yeah. Thanks."

"Mrs. Balzli is waiting in the driveway," Pru said gently.

With another shy wave, Ari headed out the door. As soon as it closed, Maggie blew out a breath. "I thought we'd be on better footing by now."

"You're intimidating," Kennedy told her.

Insult whipped color into Maggie's fair cheeks. "I am not."

"You kind of are," Pru said. "It works for you. Most of the time. You're the woman who Gets Things Done."

"Pru is the warm, fuzzy one," Kennedy said.

"What about you?" Maggie demanded. Was that jealousy in her tone?

"I'm the most like Ari. She relates to me."

An almost imperceptible shudder passed over Maggie, as if perishing the thought of having another sister like Kennedy. "Well, it's good she'll open up to at least some of us." Turning on heel, she strode with purpose into the kitchen.

Kennedy and Pru exchanged a look. "Business mode," Kennedy murmured. Not quite ready to face whatever her middle sister wanted to discuss, she said, "I'll be right back. Need to run upstairs for a minute."

It was a foolish and unnecessary delay, but she retreated to her room, pulling out her laptop and compulsively checking email. Maybe there'd be something from Flynn.

But it wasn't email from Flynn that snagged her attention. It was an email from the book editor.

Hey Kennedy,

I was just following up on our conversation from a few weeks ago. Tried to call you at the pub and was referred to one Flynn Bohannon. He told me about your mother. I'm so very sorry for your loss. I know you're dealing with a lot, but I just wanted to keep the lines of communication open. Still very interested in the book project, and the powers that be are pumped. Ready and willing to discuss when you're in a better place.

Enthusiastically yours,

Elena Beckhoff

Kennedy read the email through twice more, feeling her pulse jitter. The whole thing was still on the table. Her eyes fell on the stack of scrapbooks piled on a chair in the corner. She'd almost swear she caught a whiff of violets from that direction. Mom would want her to do this. Or at least talk to the woman about it more in depth. Deciding that was scarier than whatever Maggie wanted to discuss, Kennedy shut the laptop and went back downstairs.

She found Maggie fiddling with the coffee pot instead of ready to get down to brass tacks. Needing something to do herself to dispel the nervous energy coursing through her from the email, Kennedy moved to tackle the breakfast dishes.

"So how did your date with Xander go last night?" The question itself wasn't unexpected. That it came from Maggie was.

"Fine." Which told them exactly nothing.

One fair brow winged up. "You were home awfully late for it to just be fine."

Kennedy plunged her hands into the sink and began scrubbing at the sausage drippings in the skillet. "I didn't sleep with him, if that's what you're asking." Not for lack of trying. There was no sense in being embarrassed by that. His rejection had nothing to do with not wanting her. That much had been clear.

But instead of taking what she'd offered, he'd denied his own needs and given her what she'd needed. He'd listened. He'd defended. In the face of lackluster support from her family, Xander's unwavering belief was humbling. Beyond that, he'd given her something infinitely more precious. A second chance.

There'd been more to his kiss, more to his touch last night than the old, familiar heat and affection. Like stumbling across a unicorn on a hike, she didn't want to look too closely, lest it disappear. Whatever it was left her feeling shaky and fragile inside, and so very, very needy. She didn't know how it could work, didn't know if she'd ever be free of the ghosts from her past. But for the first time she felt brave enough to try. To have Xander back, she'd be willing to endure almost anything.

From the other side of the room, Pru studied her with a serious expression that had discomfort crawling up Kennedy's spine.

"So we had business to discuss?" she prompted. Might as well take the pressure off herself somehow.

Maggie poured them all fresh cups of coffee and gestured to

the big farmhouse table. Kennedy set the clean dishes in the dish drainer, and they took their seats.

"Do we need to call Athena, get her on speakerphone?" Pru asked.

"I already talked to her about this on the drive to the airport yesterday."

"And you waited to loop us in why?" Kennedy asked.

"You were off with Xander, and I wanted to have this discussion with Ari out of the house."

That sobered Kennedy right up. "What's going on, Maggie?"

"As you know, I've been in close contact with Robert about the state of Mom's finances. In particular the trust responsible for paying the property taxes, upkeep on the house, and other expenses associated with having this much acreage." She paused and sipped at the coffee. "It seems Mom took a great deal out of the trust over the last decade or so to pay for college expenses, not only for us, but for quite a few other fosters."

Pru's hands laced around her coffee mug. "How much?"

"A lot. Which would have been bad enough but could've been recouped. Except the bottom fell out of the stock market last year."

"So how much is left?" Kennedy asked.

"Not even enough to pay off the lien. It may rebound some eventually, but given the economic forecast for the country the next few years, we're going to be on our own covering all those expenses, for a while at least."

Kennedy read between the lines. "So we could lose the house."

"It's not quite that dire yet. Athena and I will help as much as we can financially."

Pru wasn't rolling in it with her massage business, and, of course, Maggie assumed Kennedy had nothing to contribute financially after the way she'd lived. She had some, but given the scope of what they needed, it might as well have been nothing.

"Why do you have that tone like there's more bad news?" she asked.

"Because there is."

"There's something worse than possibly losing the house?" Pru asked.

"Mom's life insurance had lapsed. The renewal got lost in the shuffle while she was dealing with the adoption, so there won't be anything incoming there either."

Pru just closed her eyes. "We were counting on that."

"The important thing that Robert keeps emphasizing is that with the probate, we have time to come up with some kind of a plan. I've got to catch up on work as soon as I get back to L.A., but I'll keep working on this. Meanwhile, it might be worth going through the loft more thoroughly to see if there really are any antiques up there worth anything. It wouldn't make much of a dent, but it would give a little bit of a buffer for normal expenses."

"We're not so bad off," Pru insisted. "Now that I'm back to work, I've got steady income again."

"And I'm not destitute, despite what you may think," Kennedy said. "I haven't been a leech before, and I'm not going to start now."

Maggie looked chagrined. "I don't think you're a leech. And if I've made you feel like I do, I'm sorry. This whole situation has me upset."

"I know. There are a lot of unknowns and a great deal of this is entirely out of your control. You don't handle that well." Understatement of the century. "But there's one thing I handle better than anyone else in this family—and that's maintaining the optimism that it will all turn out all right in the end, even if we don't know how. I've lived my life by that for ten years, and I haven't been wrong yet. I don't plan to start now."

"I don't think optimism is going to carry the day here."

"My sunny, can-do attitude isn't the only thing I plan to throw at this situation. I'm going to brainstorm and help you come up with a plan." Kennedy rolled on before Maggie could utter the *Thanks, but no thanks* on her tongue. "I know I don't have your business training or financial knowledge, but I do have a lot of life experience in a lot of different areas. It may be that I can think of something outside the box."

She thought of the book option. Yeah, that was definitely outside the box. But when and if that happened, it would be a long time in the future. As little as she knew about publishing, even she was aware it was a slow process. They needed an influx of cash now.

Maggie was silent a moment. "Well, nothing has popped for me inside the box, so go for it."

"I intend to. And in the meantime, I'm headed into town." Kennedy shoved back from the table.

"What? Now?"

"Yes, now."

"For what?"

"I'm going to find a job."

∼

STONE COUNTY ENCOMPASSED two-hundred square miles of mountain and valley. Xander spent a lot of his time driving from one end to the other, answering calls, working cases. But at least two or three times a week, he liked to do a foot patrol of downtown Eden's Ridge. To his mind, it was good to be a visible presence—not that the Ridge suffered from much in the way of crime to begin with. Beyond that, he just liked getting out from behind his desk or the wheel of his department cruiser to move.

Today was especially nice, with the weather warming on up to true spring and flowers nodding in the breeze from various pots and planters in front of the shops on Main Street. It was the kind of day worth grabbing take out from Crystal's Diner and finding a bench somewhere to soak up some sun. That idea took on even more appeal as he spotted Kennedy striding down the sidewalk from the opposite direction. Her blonde ponytail bobbed back and forth with her purposeful stride—as close to Woman On A Mission as she ever really got.

Checking traffic, he crossed over to intercept her. "Fancy meeting you here."

Her smile was quick and warm. "Well, you've just made my trip to town doubly worthwhile."

"Yeah? What'd you come in for?"

"Job hunting."

"Already? I'd figured you'd take a little more time to settle in."

The smiled turned into more of a wince. "Well, things are a little dicey with the house and the rest of our property. It seems Mom has been robbing the trust that pays for it to hand out college educations. A lot of them. So we're working on figuring the finances out and how we're going to pay for upkeep. In the meantime, that means we're all working girls. Hence, job hunting."

"Success?" he asked, though he knew the answer from her faintly triumphant expression.

"You're looking at the new bartender at Elvira's Tavern. It may not be glamorous, but, it's something I'm good at that'll bring in a steady paycheck."

"What happened to Denver?"

"He wanted to make me just a waitress. They're short-staffed, apparently, but then I got behind the taps and worked some magic. He's decided he doesn't need to work every blessed night of the week. With me on board, he's got more free time to woo Misty Pennebaker."

Xander went brows up. "He tell you all that?"

"Oh no. The gossip portion of that was opining from Trish Morgan. I think I like her better now than I did in high school. Anyway, I have no idea who Misty Pennebaker is, but I hope she digs the strong, silent type, because Denver seems like a really good guy."

Xander pointed across the street to the new-agey curiosity and florist shop. "Misty owns Moonbeams and Sweet Dreams over there. Relatively new to the Ridge. Been here maybe three years now, I think."

As they watched, Misty herself emerged from the shop, a watering can in hand and what appeared to be a crown of daisies in her dark brown hair. Her long, flowing skirts swished as she bent to water the flowers rioting in profusion from the boxes out front. The flower child and the ex-biker. Now there was a romance he wouldn't have called.

Apparently following the same line of thought, Kennedy muttered, "It'll be interesting to be a fly on the wall for that one."

"Yep."

"Anyway, as of tomorrow night, I should be gainfully employed."

"That should make Maggie happy."

"Happy or not, she heads back to L.A. today. Since things are not awesome with the financial situation of Mom's estate, she's wigging. And her stress over it is stressing us out. It'll be good to be down to just Pru and Ari for a little while."

"You had lunch yet?" Xander asked.

"I have not."

"Buy you some."

"If it comes with your charming company, the answer's yes."

"Let's walk on down to Crystal's."

Kennedy fell into step beside him. "Do they still have the grilled mac 'n cheese sandwich?"

"Of course. It's a diner staple."

"It's nice to know some things stay the same. I've been really surprised by all the new businesses in town. Main Street has a whole extra block than when I left, and it seems like a bunch of the businesses have changed over."

Because he couldn't think of a good reason not to, Xander took her hand. She glanced up at him, the corners of her mouth tipping up in a way that made him want to kiss her. Eyes twinkling, as if she knew exactly what he was thinking, she swung their joined hands in a wide arc, as they used to back in high school.

"We've had a little bit of growth. There are those trying to bring tourism to the Ridge. We get dribs and drabs of people. Lot of hikers. Folks doing antiquing. But the powers that be are wanting to do a big push for more since the Gatlinburg fires. It's kinda mercenary, trying to capitalize on their misfortune, but it's probably the best shot we've got. There's even been some talk of building a resort."

"A resort? In Eden's Ridge?"

He shrugged. "Tourism and resorts are big business down in Gatlinburg and Pigeon Forge. Mountain vacations and a little luxury for common folks."

"Definitely not arguing that point. But wouldn't a resort be too late to take advantage of the fires? I mean, they'd have to build it, so that puts the whole thing off into next year at the earliest."

"Maybe. There have been a growing number of rental cabins being built, and quite a few people are taking advantage of AirBnB. It's a small start, but it's a start getting people here. If the town makes a good impression, people are liable to come back. Especially people who don't like all the congestion and tourist trap feel of Gatlinburg."

She hummed a considering noise. "I'll have to research what's here and make a post about it on my travel blog."

"Your what now?"

"My travel blog. It's monetized. That's part of how I've funded my travel all these years. By chronicling all the places I've lived and visited and talking about how to travel affordably. It's not huge, but it's got a pretty decent following. And somebody might find the Ridge that way."

And she just kept surprising him with her resourcefulness.

Xander tugged open the door to the diner. "Your sisters know about that?"

"It's never come up. I started it more for me, to keep up with where I went. And it just kind of grew." She made a beeline for their old booth by the window.

"What's it called?"

"Not All Who Wander."

"Because you weren't lost."

Kennedy inclined her head. She plucked a menu from the holder on the table and began to scan it.

In his pocket, Xander's phone began to vibrate. He fished it out and checked the display. His father. No way in hell was he answering that right now. If it were an actual emergency, he'd be hearing from Essie as dispatch over the radio. More likely, somebody saw him and Kennedy together and told Buck. Sending the call to voicemail, Xander shoved it back into his pocket.

Nicky Blue, daughter of the diner's namesake, swung by their table, order pad in hand. "What can I get you, Deputy?"

"I'll take the meatloaf special."

The girl scribbled it down. "And you?" She turned curious eyes on Kennedy.

"The grilled mac 'n cheese sandwich with a pile of curly fries. And a root beer."

"Comin' right up." She started to turn away but Xander stopped her.

"Let's add an Oreo milkshake to that, too. Two straws." Very deliberately, he reached across the table to tangle his fingers with Kennedy's.

Nicky's brows disappeared beneath her teased bangs. "Yes, sir."

Kennedy's lips twitched as the waitress disappeared into the kitchen. "Felt like making an announcement, huh?"

"Seemed more expedient to get the word out." He met her gaze. "Is that a problem for you?"

She shook her head and squeezed his hand. "No problem at all."

"So. Blogger, huh?" He pulled his phone back out and opened a browser, running a quick Google search for Not All Who Wander.

A blush crawled up Kennedy's cheeks. "Don't go look it up."

"Why not?"

"I don't know. It feels weird to have anybody from home know about it. It's weird having anybody important know about it."

There was something in her tone that had him studying her face. She was looking down at their joined hands, chewing the inside of her lip in an old gesture that told him she was worried about something.

"Who else knows about it?"

She lifted her gaze to his before glancing around the diner to see that no one was close. When she spoke, her voice was low. "There's this editor. She wants to talk to me about turning the whole thing into a book."

"That's awesome!"

Her shoulders lifted in a half-hearted shrug that wasn't near as casual as she wanted it to be. "I don't know. It all happened before Mom died. I haven't given any kind of answer, but she emailed me about it again this morning."

"Well, of course you should do it. Joan would've been tickled pink at the idea of you being an author."

"I'm not an author."

The site loaded on his phone, and he saw the note in the banner. "Pretty sure you wouldn't be award-winning if you weren't."

Kennedy dropped her eyes again. "It was just some web award. Nobody outside the industry would've heard of it."

Xander set the phone aside and took her other hand. "Hey, why are you minimizing everything you've accomplished? You did all this, on your own, and it's amazing. Imagine what you could do with the backing of a publisher. You could make a career of this."

As soon as the words were out of his mouth, he realized what he was suggesting. Kennedy could have a career as a professional travel writer. Which meant she'd have to travel. She could hardly do something like that from the Ridge. He'd only just gotten her back and here he was encouraging her to leave again—albeit indirectly. That was fucked up.

She shrugged again. "I can't be a travel writer without traveling, and I'm needed here."

Which wasn't at all the same thing as *I don't want to be a travel writer.*

But Xander shoved down the flutter of panic in his gut that she'd disappear on him. She was committed to being here. For Ari and Pru and, at least in part, for him. She needed someone to support her absolutely. She wasn't getting that from her sisters. Even if she told them about the opportunity, he doubted they'd rave about it. They were the ones who'd made her feel like a screw up again since she came back, erasing the easy confidence she'd had when he first saw her at the cemetery. He wanted to give that back to her.

So he squeezed her hand and forced a smile. "Maybe don't think about it in broad strokes of career. Talk to her about what you can do with what you've already written, the places you've already been. You owe it to yourself to explore the option."

As Nicky came back with their lunch, Kennedy pulled her hand from his and leaned back to make room for the plate. "I'll think about it."

CHAPTER 10

IF EDEN'S RIDGE WANTED to bring tourism in, they needed a better web presence. That was Kennedy's estimation after she spent some time Googling to see what services and accommodations were available. The information that was out there was spotty and disconnected. The town itself needed something dedicated to tourism to connect prospective visitors with all the various options. But despite the less than stellar representation, there *was* the seed of tourism out there. Tourism in the Ridge.

She could just hear Athena scoffing at the idea, as she'd scoffed at the suggestion that anyone would think of Pru's new workspace as a mini-spa. But the kind of people who'd be drawn to a place like Eden's Ridge absolutely weren't the demographic her sister was used to serving in her upscale Chicago restaurant. They weren't celebrities, or rich women with purse dogs, or snobby businessmen, who probably took off to St. Moritz on a whim—Kennedy knew that type and had catered to them often in various capacities over the years. The kind of people who'd be drawn to Eden's Ridge were, as Xander had said, everyday folks.

The same demographic who were accustomed to vacationing in Gatlinburg.

The whole thing had Kennedy thinking.

People would be looking to alternatives to Gatlinburg, while it was being rebuilt. That meant the need, the prospective market, was ripe now—not next year or years down the line, once a full resort could be built. Some would take advantage of the rental cabins in the area, but others would be looking for something with a bit more service and pampering. The kind of experience they'd find at a cozy bed and breakfast.

And here they sat with this big, mostly empty house...

It was a lunatic idea. Kennedy knew that. But it hadn't stopped her from nabbing a notepad and conducting her own evaluation of the possibilities. She walked through the freshly cleaned rooms, looking with new eyes, eyes that had seen countless B and Bs over the years, making note of which rooms could easily be converted for prospective guests. There weren't en suite bathrooms for every room, and that would be an issue for some people. But she'd stayed in plenty of B and Bs in other parts of the world where sharing was the norm. And with more people in the US using services like AirBnB, there was a segment of travelers who were getting more accustomed to that sort of arrangement.

Fresh coats of paint everywhere, for sure. A house didn't serve as hub for dozens of kids over the years without taking something of a beating. But it had good bones and a lot of Victorian charm. Fresh linens for all the beds. The current hodge podge of comforters, quilts, and bedspreads might be okay with a good washing. And she was pretty sure she'd seen a trunk of other quilts up in the hay loft. Most of the furniture was in good shape. A good cleaning with lemon oil would take care of most of it, and the few pieces that looked too rough could be painted shabby chic style. That would suit a quaint, Southern inn.

Kennedy made notes on her pad.

Inquire about local art for the walls. If they could work up an actual clientele, they could serve as another point of sale for the artists. Make them fall in love with the house, the area, and want to take a piece of their stay home.

With a lot of planning, a lot of prep, it could work. She knew it could. The idea gave her a buzz of challenge. She could do this and it would be a way to finally contribute, not only to her family, but to the community. She could make her mark.

"Whatcha doing?"

Kennedy turned to find Ari in the doorway. "Hey. How was school?"

The girl jerked her too thin shoulders. "Was okay, I guess. What are you doing up here?" she asked again.

"Dreaming big."

A spark of interest lit those big, brown eyes. "Yeah? What about?"

Kennedy hesitated. Maggie had deliberately kept Ari out of the loop of the finance discussion. She hadn't wanted to worry the girl unnecessarily, especially with Ari's own fate up in the air. Kennedy understood that. But she also understood how frustrating and upsetting it was to be kept ignorant of details that could absolutely impact your life. Especially as it was likely she knew more than they were aware of. Mom had often said, "Little bunnies have big ears."

Kennedy sat on the bed and patted the mattress beside her. "Come sit for a bit."

Ari's eyes shuttered, that careful blanking of expression Kennedy had, herself, perfected at an early age. Never show vulnerability. Especially when shit was about to hit the fan. But she sat curling her feet up beneath her. "Is something wrong?"

"Not exactly. Can you keep a secret?"

"Sure."

"So you know we've been dealing with all the details of

Mom's estate. The four of us are equal owners of the house, the property, and all that."

Ari's eyes widened. "Do Athena and Maggie want to sell?"

"No! No, no. Nothing like that. But maintaining a property this size is expensive. Most of the costs used to be covered by a trust, but for a lot of complicated reasons, that's not an option right now, so we have to find a way to pay for stuff like property taxes and upkeep. And that's what I'm dreaming about. A way to make the house pay for itself."

The girl frowned. "How?"

"I think we could turn it into an inn." She felt a snap of excitement in her blood just saying it aloud.

"Like a hotel?"

"Much smaller than that. A bed and breakfast. We've got all this space that no one's using, all these bedrooms. The house would need a bit of spiffing up, but we could rent out some of the rooms to tourists, provide them a meal or two. What do you think? How would you feel about having strangers in the house?"

Unlike a lot of her predecessors, Ari hadn't had a constantly rotating parade of other fosters going through the house during her time here. Mom had been dialing back for the last couple of years, as she'd gotten older. But Kennedy liked people, liked the idea of the house still being used.

"I think," Ari said slowly, "that Joan would've liked the idea."

"Did you know she used to call this place The Misfit Inn? Where misfits of all ages and types could find a home."

"She was good at that. At making us feel at home. If we could do something like that for other people, even on a temporary basis, it feels like maybe that would be a way to kind of keep her here with us."

"*Yes.*" Kennedy hugged Ari. "Yes, that's it exactly. But would you be okay with it?"

"Does it matter what I think? Joan's gone, so this isn't really my home anymore."

Kennedy felt her heart crack in two. "This *is* your home. You are a Reynolds. That's what Mom wanted. We just have to finish sorting out all the legal crap. And, yeah, it might get messy because this is an unusual situation, but all four of us will fight for you. You're family."

Ari's chin wobbled and her eyes went a bit glassy. "Okay then." She rubbed an impatient hand over her face and looked around the room. "What kind of changes would it take?"

"I'm still working on all that. I don't want to present it to my sisters until I have all the details worked out for how it could work, so let's keep this between us for now. Our little secret."

"I can do that."

"Great." Kennedy stood. "Want to go play in the hay loft to see what kind of treasures we could repurpose from up there?"

A slow smile spread across Ari's face. "That sounds like fun."

~

"You're in a good mood," Jarvis observed.

"Am I?" Xander asked, aware that he'd come back to work whistling.

"You're smiling while doing paperwork."

He'd had what felt like a permanent grin stuck on his face since lunch. It probably made him look like a total love-struck goofball, but what did he care? He was. "Guess I am. No reason not to be in a good mood. It's a beautiful day, and the citizens of our fine county have been behaving themselves."

"That the only reason?" Essie asked, her eyes bright with mischief and an unabashed hope.

"Might not be," Xander conceded.

"Heard you were sharing a milkshake with Kennedy up at Crystal's earlier. In your old booth."

"So we were," he said easily. He'd wanted the word spread quickly. Mission accomplished. And he couldn't really resent

Essie's interest. He knew she'd been rooting for them to get back together.

"Y'all worked out your differences?" Jarvis asked carefully.

"We did."

"She told you why she left?" Essie asked.

"She did. Not that it's any of y'all's business. More importantly, she's home to stay."

"Good for her," Essie declared, obviously relieved. "I never agreed with Buck bullying her out of town."

Xander felt the smile on his face turn brittle. "I'm sorry, what?"

Panic skittered over Essie's face, the kind of panic Xander was used to seeing in suspects who'd accidentally said too much. "I, um..."

He'd assumed her leaving was all about him, about the fight they'd had. Kennedy hadn't said otherwise. But deep down, he'd wondered if there'd been more keeping her away.

"Essie, you know something about why Kennedy left. What is it?"

"I—oh dear." Her wrinkled cheeks flushed, then went pale. "If she didn't tell you herself..."

He rose from his desk and advanced on the dispatcher, consciously shifting into interrogation mode. "What do you know?"

Essie cast a nervous glance toward Buck's office.

"He's not here right now. And you're going to tell me."

"Xander, I'm not sure I should—"

"This is about Kennedy. Which makes this about me. Whatever it is I don't know can impact our relationship. I can't deal with it if I don't know."

Another look toward his father's office.

"This won't come back on you. I swear it."

Her painted lips trembled, but she nodded once. "On the night of your high school graduation, Kennedy was pulled over in a routine roadblock. You know how they do, trying to catch the kids drinking and whatnot."

"Kennedy hadn't been drinking." Xander knew that definitively because he had, and she'd been designated driver. This must've happened after she dropped him home.

"No, but, well, she had drugs in the car."

"She *what?*" That made absolutely no sense. Kennedy never did drugs. She'd never even so much as smoked.

"Jim brought her in," Essie said, referring to Xander's predecessor. "Buck was here, and he said he'd handle it. He took her into interrogation. I didn't like the look on his face, so I went back to the locker room to listen through the ducts."

Now was not the time to chastise her for listening in on confidential interrogations.

"He asked her about them, where they'd come from. She said they weren't hers. That some kids at a party she'd gone to were planning to use them, and she knew that was stupid, so she took them and intended to get rid of them before anybody could hurt themselves."

Now that sounded like something she'd do.

"And then?"

"He asked her to name names. Say who all was at the party, who she'd gotten the drugs from. She wouldn't do it."

Because he'd been at that party. So had all their closest friends and a fair chunk of the senior class. Kennedy was no sellout.

"Buck got mad then. He hated that drugs had gotten into our county, turned into a problem. Took it as a personal attack. I knew he didn't like her. But I never thought he'd—"

A sick feeling took up residence in Xander's gut. "He what, Essie?"

"He told her it didn't matter if she named other names, he had her on felony possession charges with intent to distribute, and he…he used it to blackmail her."

"That's bullshit. Kennedy never did drugs. She didn't even drink."

"I'm just telling you what I heard. The drugs were in her car. Jim was very clear about that."

And given the laws in Tennessee, she could be charged, whether they'd been hers or not. But officers had room for discretion, as did judges, to look at the realities of each individual case.

"You said he blackmailed her. How?"

"Everybody knows Joan had a zero tolerance policy for criminal behavior. He played on her fear, made her believe that this whole thing would make Joan kick her out. She was eighteen, a legal adult. Joan didn't have to be responsible for her anymore. Scared that poor girl to death. But he said he'd make her a deal. He'd see that all the charges went away if she left town, without you. He made it clear the deal only stayed in place so long as she stayed gone."

Xander's hands curled to useless fists as shock slid into anger. His father had never liked Kennedy, but he never would have believed Buck would use his position as Sheriff to do something like this. "Why didn't you say anything?"

Essie knotted her hands and worried the lipstick off her bottom lip. She seemed to have aged a decade over the past few minutes. "I couldn't risk my job. Not with Henry being in chemo. And honestly, I never dreamed she'd really do it. Everybody could see how much she loved you, and I thought she'd fight. She was never the type to just roll over when someone attacked her. So when she left, it was a shock. And then she stayed gone and...I didn't want to bring it up and hurt you more."

Xander's blood was boiling, but he struggled to keep himself in check. This wasn't Essie's fault. "What happened to the case file?"

"There wasn't one. She was never formally arrested."

"What about the evidence? Was it ever sent off to the lab for analysis?"

"A few months later it was, when a similar stash was found. Arrests were made. It was after you'd left for college."

"And what was it?"

"I don't remember."

"Who was arrested? Pull up the damned file." Xander knew he was snarling, but everything he'd believed for ten years was wrong and he needed to see how bad this really was.

With shaking hands, Essie checked the computer, then went to pull a file from the cabinet.

He yanked it from her and flipped to the lab report. The way the laws were written, charges were the same whether the drugs were marijuana or something harder. He had to know what the hell she'd been caught with, what exactly his father had been sitting on for years. He read the lab report through, then read it a second time as relief and fury hit him in equal measure.

Coral plants. Kennedy had been threatened with felony drug possession over *coral plants*. Not even a legitimate drug. Even if he'd charged her, the charges wouldn't have held up.

Without another word, he strode to his desk and snatched up his keys.

"Where are you going?" Essie's worried voice floated after him.

"To talk to my father."

Buck had taken the afternoon off for a doctor's check-up, so he'd be home now. Xander intended to corner the bear in his den.

Why the hell hadn't Kennedy told him? He could see why she hadn't told him then. She'd been running scared. But now? She'd had every opportunity to tell him the truth when he'd apologized for the fight. Every chance to tell him it wasn't his fault. Instead, she'd continued to lie about it.

His mother's car was in the garage when he pulled up to the house where he'd grown up. Did she know what his father had done? Xander slammed the door of the car and stalked into the house without knocking. Buck was watching ESPN in his favorite recliner.

"Xander. What are you doing—"

"You son of a bitch."

Buck's brows drew down like thunderclouds. "Now hold on a damned minute."

Mom hurried into the room, a kitchen towel clutched in her hands. "Xander? What's going on?"

"Did you know? Did you know he blackmailed Kennedy with some bogus felony drug charges to leave town and stay the hell away from me?"

His mother's mouth dropped open. "Buck?"

"They weren't bogus charges. She was picked up at a road block with a bag of drugs in her car."

"It was fucking *coral plants*. Not even marijuana. Don't even try to lie to me. I saw the lab reports from the bust you made on Nelson Rimer."

"Didn't know that at the time," Buck defended. "And she'd been at a party with minors."

"She'd been at a party with *me* and the entire senior class. Where she was the designated driver and one of the only sober people there. And even if she was found with drugs in her car, the likelihood that they were hers was nil. She had no history of drug or alcohol use. No criminal record of any kind. She wouldn't, not only because was she a good girl, but she would never have done anything to risk Joan's wrath. And you knew that. You knew and you fucking well used that against her."

An ugly flush was rising up his father's face. "She tell you that?"

Conscious of protecting Essie as he'd promised, Xander ignored the question. "It doesn't matter how I found out. Why would you do that? Why would you go to such lengths to get rid of her?"

"Because I didn't want to lose you," Buck hollered back. He was red all the way up to his hairline and he was breathing hard. "You would've followed that girl anywhere, whether it made any goddamned sense or not. And if you'd left, you'd have stayed gone." He made an obvious effort to calm himself. "I only wanted what's best for you, son. She was bad news."

"She was an innocent girl. You used your authority in a wholly unethical fashion and straight up lied to her, emotionally manipulating her for your own sick ends." Rage made him half blind. "You're a disgrace to the badge."

"It's not my proudest moment, I admit, but how much did she really love you if she stayed away all these years?"

The blow struck Xander somewhere around his heart. It was a question that had been circling around beneath the surface of his brain for days. And one he was damned well going to get an answer to.

"It's not about how much she loved me. It's about how much I loved her. How you railroaded out of town the only woman I have ever loved and made her stay gone for ten goddamned years. How is that what's best for me? It's only what's best for you."

His mother took a step closer, the towel knotted in her hands. In contrast to Buck's face, hers had gone chalk white. "Let's everybody take a deep breath."

Xander barely spared her a glance. All his focus, all his rage was on his father. "You cut her off from the only family she had all this time. For the rest of her mother's life. Years she's never going to get back, and time she didn't deserve to lose because you didn't approve of her as a girlfriend."

"Son—"

But Xander couldn't hear it. He took a step backward. "Fuck you, Dad. You aren't the man I thought you were. Stay the hell away from me and from Kennedy."

Turning on heel, he stalked back out of the house.

CHAPTER 11

THE HOUSE WAS BLESSEDLY empty, at last. It had taken some creative persuasion on Kennedy's part to convince Ari and Pru to go on to the movies without her. Not that she minded being in a house with other people. She was a social person by nature, and this house never felt quite right unless there were several people around. But she'd wanted some time to begin putting all the details of her plan together without drawing Pru's curiosity. And to write the email to Elena she'd been composing in the back of her mind all afternoon. After Xander's enthusiastic support, she'd finally taken the plunge and emailed back that she was interested in further discussion of the possibility of a book. It wasn't a done deal by any means, but Elena had already emailed back to set up a call to talk about details. Caught up in equal parts excitement and terror, Kennedy had set that aside to focus on her business plan for the inn.

The living room was covered in lists. It looked like her legal pad had vomited pages on every horizontal surface. The coffee table, the chairs, the end of the sofa. Kennedy was on the verge of making a list of her lists, just to keep things straight. Which rooms could be turned over to guests, which would remain family space. Which areas of the house would be public, which would be private. Lists of supplies to price. More lists of furniture to be swapped out from the barn. Lists of details associated with building a website. If Maggie had put something like this together, it'd be all neat and orderly, organized in spreadsheets, with all kinds of estimates and profit and loss statements. That was what she responded to. So once Kennedy finished gathering all her details, she'd have to translate it into the language her sister spoke, if she wanted to be taken seriously. God help her.

But Kennedy could do it. She *would* do it. She might not have the business degree to go along with the presentation, but she'd learned a helluva lot more than how to do menial labor in all the jobs she'd worked. She had a solid and agile mind. She just learned better on the job than from a book or a classroom. And she intended to prove that she had something to offer this family.

A knock on the door dragged her away from all her lists. The vague sense of irritation fled as she saw the familiar broad shoulders through the sidelight.

"Xander!" The instant spurt of pleasure faded as she registered the hard set of his jaw, the glittering temper in his eyes. "What's wrong?"

He didn't wait for an invitation before stalking past her. He'd changed to street clothes, so he wasn't coming straight from work. Fury radiated off him like heat waves. The moment he turned those hard, dark eyes on her, Kennedy went cold.

"Why didn't you tell me?" His quiet, deadly tone was more terrifying than any shout.

"Tell you what?" But she knew. Deep down in her gut, she knew that somehow he'd found out about what had really happened the night she left Eden's Ridge.

"The truth. About why you really left. I asked you for honesty, Kennedy."

Her heart beat thick and fast and her knees went loose, as she felt everything she'd wanted begin to tip out of her grasp. "I...I couldn't. Those were the terms I agreed to." She hated that her voice trembled, hated that she'd been caught in this lie of omission.

"Why?"

"How could I tell you I'd been facing drug charges? Your father had me over a barrel. He didn't give me a choice. Not really."

Xander's nostrils flared. "Tell me what really happened that night. All of it."

She'd done everything in her power to avoid this moment, but she knew she owed him this or she'd lose him for sure. "When we were at the party that night, I overheard a bunch of people planning on getting high and going over to Peter Bevridge's house. They wanted to take out his dad's gun collection to shoot up beer bottles." She'd tried so hard not to think of it. To block the entire horrible experience out of her mind. But she remembered the scents of alcohol, the too loud music and the press of people as everyone gave in to the insanity of finally being free of mandatory education. "Jason Mather was mouthing off about some weed that he'd scored. There was already a lot of drinking going on, and I figured the whole thing was a recipe for somebody getting killed. So, while everybody was distracted, I hid their car keys and stole Jason's bag. It was loaded with weed. Too much to just flush down the toilet without risking it getting stopped up. I figured I'd find some other way to get rid of it after I dropped you off at home. I didn't count on the road block." She still remembered the flashlight blinding her before Deputy Bailey shone it into the back seat. The zipper on Jason's bag had been busted. After the fight with Xander, she'd forgotten all about the drugs.

"I got hauled in and your father took me into interrogation. I explained what had happened, but he didn't believe me. I could see that before I'd even finished. Then he asked for names, for who was at the party. And I—I didn't want to get every single person I knew in trouble. Especially you. Your dad would've absolutely had a conniption fit if he knew you'd been drinking. I was trying to think of who to tell him, if anybody, but then he said it didn't matter whether I cooperated or not because he had me on felony charges."

Xander interrupted. "Did anyone ever read you your rights?"

"I—" Had they? That part of the night had been something of a blur. She'd been too shell-shocked at the prospect of a felony to absorb a lot of what came after. "I don't remember. I don't think we got to that part."

A muscle jumped in his jaw. "Keep going."

Kennedy tucked her icy hands beneath her armpits in a vain attempt to warm them. "All I could think about was protecting you and what Mom would say. How upset and disappointed she'd be. It was the one thing she never, ever tolerated out of any of us. You know Jeanette got kicked out for bringing pot into the house. I guess your dad could see I was scared shitless. And then he said he'd make me a deal. He could make all this go away, waive the charges so Mom would never know, as long as I left town immediately without contacting you." It had been like taking a knife to the gut. A choice that had been no choice. "You were the good son, who'd never party with a bad girl like me, and he wanted me out of your life. No longer a temptation. He'd hang on to the file, and if I ever came back, ever contacted you again, he'd use it. So I took the deal. He drove me to the bus station in Johnson City himself."

Her throat wanted to close up at the look of utter betrayal on Xander's face.

She was crying again, big, fat tears rolling down her cheeks. "I'm sorry. I'm so sorry. It was never that I didn't love you. But I couldn't lose my family. I just...couldn't. And I couldn't go to jail for something I didn't do."

Xander pinched the bridge of his nose. "You wouldn't have gone to jail. The charges were bullshit."

Kennedy stared at him. "What?"

"You were never formally arrested. You weren't properly mirandized. Even if you had been, a judge would have taken your history into account, the fact that you didn't drink or smoke or do drugs. At most, you would've faced a fine. Buck saw an opportunity to box you into a corner, to manipulate you, and he took it." His hands were curled into fists and he looked ready to drive one through the nearest wall. "The son of a bitch split us up with some goddamned coral plants. It wasn't even real drugs."

The implications of that cut the knees right out from under her. She sank to the rug, her legs just folding like a house of cards. She'd been played. She'd been played, and she'd lost everything. Him. Her family. Years she could've spent with her mother.

Xander stalked to the window and back, his body snapping with barely leashed violence. "If you'd told me, I'd have rolled on every fucking person at that party. Someone else saw, someone else would've remembered, pointed fingers. The truth would've come out, and you wouldn't have had to go."

"I didn't know," she whispered. "He threatened me, and I believed him. Why wouldn't I? He's the sheriff."

"He terrorized you. I'll never forgive him for what he did to you. What he did to us." The furious words should've made her feel somewhat better. But he didn't touch her, didn't come near her, didn't do anything to comfort or say he was on her side. Instead, he paced a tight circle in front of the fireplace. "You should have told me, Kennedy. You should have fucking trusted me. Then, and when you came back."

There had to be a way to fix this, to get past the anger and make him see. "It had nothing to do with not trusting you. I started to call you, to email you a thousand times. But I didn't know what to say, and I knew that if you knew what had happened, you'd absolutely lose your shit with your dad, and then he'd know I'd broken the terms of our agreement and carry out his threat. The only reason I felt safe coming back at all was because Mom's dead and his leverage is gone."

He finally stopped his pacing and scrubbed both hands over his face. "I get why you didn't tell me ten years ago. I don't agree with it, but I get it. But as you've just pointed out, he lost his leverage when Joan died. Why the hell didn't you tell me that night at the bluff?"

This was the moment to lay everything bare. He would accept nothing less than the full truth. And yet, could they survive the truth? It was another impossible choice, and he'd backed her into a corner. Was there a chance in hell that he would do anything other than walk out of here tonight? None of her imagined reveals had ended any other way. She'd always known he'd be furious. But she had to believe, had to trust, that the man would be more forgiving than the boy.

"Apart from the fact that I had no idea the charges were phony, I couldn't just up and drop that bomb. I hadn't seen you in a decade. I didn't know where we stood. For all I knew, you hated me, and rightly so. I left you. No matter the reason, I left you. And in all that time you've had your family. They were here. And I thought that letting you preserve your relationship with them was more important. I know exactly what it's like to lose that, and I didn't want that for you. You'd already lost me. I didn't matter."

The silence spun on and her stomach hollowed out. *Say something. Tell me I was wrong. Tell me you still love me.*

But he only stared at her, his expression unreadable. "Would you ever have told me?"

Well, he'd asked for honesty. "I don't know," she whispered.

Xander nodded once, as if that was the deciding answer he'd needed, then headed for the door.

Kennedy scrambled up, running after him. "Where are you going?"

"Home. I can't talk about this anymore. This was a mistake. This was all a mistake."

"Xander!"

He rounded on her. "You *lied to me!* I thought for *years* that it was my fault. I blamed myself for what you put your family through. What I thought I put you through. I *told you* that at the bluff. I apologized for it. And you just stood there and let me. You didn't say a goddamned *word.*"

She flinched back. It was all imploding. Everything she'd feared from the moment he'd walked back into her life was coming to pass. Desperate, sobbing, Kennedy held out her hands toward him. "I didn't know *how!* Not without breaking my agreement with your father."

"And getting involved with me again? That wasn't a breach in that agreement?"

She'd been trying to justify this to herself, hadn't she? "I thought… My mother was already dead. My relationship with my sisters is already damaged. I thought, maybe he wouldn't act. Because there was no way he could tell you the truth either without revealing his role in all of it. Mutually assured destruction." But even to her own ears, the excuse sounded thin.

"Well congratulations. You both got exactly what you didn't want."

Before she could reach him, he'd walked out, slamming the door shut. She fumbled to yank it open, losing precious seconds before she realized he'd engaged the lock on his way out. By the time she raced onto the porch, he'd cranked the Bronco and peeled out of the drive.

Breath heaving, heart breaking, Kennedy dropped to her knees where she stood and wept as his tail-lights disappeared into the night.

∼

When the doorbell rang, Xander considered leaving it. Then he briefly considered shooting whoever was on the other side. If he couldn't drown himself in whiskey due to the possibility of being called in to handle an emergency, he should at least be able to be left alone to drink his beer and mourn the life he should've had—would have had, if not for his father. He'd taken a fucking vacation day for it.

The bell rang again.

He thought about hurling his bottle of Corona, but that'd be a shameful waste of beer.

If it was Kennedy, he wasn't ready to see her again. His stomach turned at just the thought of the look on her face when she'd said she didn't matter. How the hell could she believe that? He'd told her flat out there'd been no one else.

If it was his father, he had a fist he'd happily plant in the old man's face.

If it was anybody else, unless they brought more beer, they could go the hell away.

On the third ring, he hefted himself out of his chair. Clearly his unwelcome visitor wasn't taking the hint. Prowling across the room, he yanked open the door. His mom stood on the other side, face drawn, worry in her pretty brown eyes.

Bracing an arm against the door frame, he struggled to reel in a little of his vile temper. "I'm not in the mood for company."

"I'm not company, I'm your mother." Ignoring him and his entirely craptastic mood, she ducked under the arm he'd been using to block her entrance.

Resigned, Xander shut the door.

She scanned the room, taking in the carry out containers from Jade Palace and the nearly empty six pack.

"I know you're upset with your father—"

"If you've come here to beg for clemency on his behalf, don't waste your breath. He engaged in conduct unbecoming an officer. He used his position of authority against an innocent girl. And he fucking sent the woman I love away because of some personal vendetta. I'm not going to forgive that, Mom. I can't."

"I didn't come to ask you to forgive him. I came to check on you. What he did…" She shook her head, expression pinched with pain.

"Did you know?" Xander wasn't sure if he really wanted the confirmation that someone else in his life had betrayed him, but it was too ingrained in him to seek the truth.

"I knew he'd done…something. I never pressed him for the details. I don't know what I would have done with them if I'd known."

Xander fisted his hands again. "I could have gone after her. I could have helped her fix things with her family, made sure she was here for Maggie, that she didn't have to lose her mother."

"Yes, you could have. I have no doubt she'd have gladly welcomed you. And, after all that, you'd have left with her again and stayed gone, exactly as your father feared you would. But I don't think it would've been all sunshine and roses."

"At least we would've been together."

"Yes, but for how long? You both would've struggled, and I'm not sure your relationship could've survived it."

"You can't possibly be saying this is for the best."

"No. No I'm not saying any of this should have happened. But I am saying there's no guarantee that you'd have stayed together. You were both very different people back then. The epitome of opposites attract. Her free spirit and wildness attracted you, but I think, in the long run, it might have been hard for you to live with. You were so, so young. All this time away…it's given you both a chance to grow up. She's had ten years to find whatever she needed to find out there. And you're stable. You're both in a better place to actually see if you've got what it takes for a mature, lasting relationship now."

"I don't think that's going to happen."

"Why not? According to the rumor mill, you were already back together."

"She didn't tell me, Mom. She didn't tell me any of this, when I asked. I had to get blindsided about it from Essie."

"And you're angry with Kennedy for that?"

"I'm angry she didn't trust me."

His mother stared at him. "Honey, are you even listening to yourself? It's got nothing to do with trusting you. That poor girl was traumatized. She's been living with this secret for a decade, and I'm willing to bet she never told a soul about it because your father made sure she was too afraid to. To have all of it dragged back to light again—and I'll bet you told her it wasn't even as serious as your father made it out to be...that's got to be devastating all over again. So if you did anything other than talk to her about it and offer sympathy and support, then you deserve to be whipped."

An uncomfortable prickle of guilt worked its way past the all-consuming anger. He'd done nothing to offer sympathy or support. All he'd done was tell her the realities and snap at her about what she should have done instead. She'd cried. And then he'd laid into her about the lie.

But she hadn't lied. At least not directly. If she'd told him outright that it hadn't been his fault, that the fight had nothing to do with her leaving, he wouldn't have been able to rest until he'd known the real reason.

His mother glared at him in that way that said she knew he deserved that whipping. "Do you love her?"

"Of course, I do." He'd love her until the day he died.

"Then *fix this*. Get over your pride or hurt feelings or whatever this is. She didn't stop being who she is just because there was more to the story of why she left. She's the biggest victim in all of this because Buck didn't just drive her away from you, but from her own family. I know she kept in touch, but it wasn't the same. Not for her, not for Joan, and not for her sisters."

Xander had seen the state of her relationship with her sisters with his own eyes. Kennedy was still being punished for something that was entirely his father's fault. And still, she'd covered Buck's ass and not told Xander the truth. Because she didn't think she mattered.

He hadn't corrected her.

The leftover Chinese food turned to lead in his stomach.

"You know what I loved most about when you two were together in high school?"

"I didn't think either of you liked Kennedy." His voice came out in an awkward croak.

"We were concerned about how serious you were, so fast. Worried about what you might do with that. But I always liked her. She encouraged you to take risks. Never stupid or foolish ones, but she got you out of that totally practical, always safe routine. Not that there's anything wrong with safe, but there's so much more to life. You lost that without her."

He'd lost a lot of things without Kennedy.

"I don't think it's too late to get that back. Assuming you get your head out of your ass."

Xander tunneled his fingers through his hair. "I need to go apologize."

Marilyn nodded, satisfied. "Good. But go take a shower and change clothes first. You smell like a brewery."

CHAPTER 12

*I*N ALL HER YEARS of gainful employment, Kennedy had never felt like bailing before the first day. After the first day, sure. She'd worked a few crap jobs that were real doozies for the newbie. But an hour and a half before her first shift at Elvira's Tavern, she wanted to throw in the towel.

She wouldn't. The family needed her employed, so to work she'd go like the busy little worker bee she was. But every cell in her body wanted to curl up and hide. Because this wasn't like working the taps at O'Leary's or any of the other pubs, bars, and taverns she'd served in over the years. This was Eden's Ridge, where everybody knew her or knew of her, and they thought that gave them free license to poke into her personal life.

After Xander's display at lunch yesterday, they'd all be asking about him and whether they were back together for real. Kennedy didn't know what the hell they were, but together wasn't it. He'd made that perfectly clear when he'd stormed out.

Her heart twinged. That whole awful scene had been playing on repeat in her brain since he left. It had taken her already raw grief over her mother's death and compounded it. Since she'd come back, Xander had been an ally—almost her only ally —and now...

A soft knock sounded on her bedroom door. Kennedy managed to wipe away the latest round of tears before Pru stepped into the room.

"I'm finally finished with my last client of the day—Mrs. Haller—who really digs the new set up, by the way. You really did manage to pull off a little spa vibe in there. The essential oil diffuser was a nice touch."

"Glad she liked it." There was no hiding the croak in her voice that betrayed the crying jag.

"Honey." Pru crossed over to the bed and sat down, wrapping Kennedy in a tight hug.

That did it. That simple gesture of support broke whatever control she'd managed to cobble together. Burying her face against her sister's shoulder, she wept, pouring out all the aching pain and regret she'd been carrying around for years. She cried for the loss of her family, the loss of the life that might have been. Most of all, she cried for Xander. Because she'd blown her miracle second chance.

Pru held her through the storm, offering tissues when Kennedy had cried herself out.

"Better?"

Kennedy jerked her shoulders in a shrug. "I just hurt, Pru. Everywhere. I miss Mom so damned much. There's all this stuff I wish I could've told her. To explain..."

"Is that what this is about? Something you regret not getting to say?"

Kennedy nodded, though, of course, that wasn't the whole truth. It seemed she no longer knew how to tell the whole truth.

"She knew you loved her."

"Not that. I said that as often as I could. I just—I wish I could've told her the truth about why I left."

Pru angled her head. "You've never talked about it. With any of us."

That secret had robbed her of her family and the man she loved. She could either keep it and let the bonds between her and her sisters remain fractured, or she could break her silence and hopefully build some kind of bridge.

She took a shaky breath. "I was blackmailed into leaving."

Pru's mouth fell open. "By who?"

So Kennedy told her. All of it, including what she now knew about how none of it had to be that way. And the airing of the secret was like drawing poison out of some wound she'd been carrying around for years. It hurt like a son of a bitch, but at the end she felt like she was bleeding clean. Like maybe it was the first step in starting to heal.

"That's reprehensible! He should be arrested! Sued. Something!"

"I'm sure it's far too late for whatever recourse might have been available."

"But he lied!"

"Cops do it all the time in interrogation. At least if all the books and movies are to be believed. I was young and naive, and he played on that. I don't think there's any law against it."

"There is no excuse for what he did," Pru declared.

"No. No I'm not defending him. I'm still wrapping my head around the fact that none of it was real. There are all these what-ifs rolling around in my head, and they're just making me sick."

"Why didn't you ever tell any of us?" Pru asked. "I mean, I understand initially, but later. You've taken so much flack for how you've lived all these years, and none of us ever knew the why."

"Because I was afraid. I have no idea what the statute of limitations is on that kind of crime, and legal ramifications aside, I was terrified that if I told, that you wouldn't believe me either, and I'd end up getting kicked out of the family completely."

"Kennedy." Pru's hug was fierce, almost punishing in its intensity. "You are a Reynolds. You've been a Reynolds from the moment Mom signed those adoption papers. You didn't have to do anything to earn that. Mom loved you. We all love you. You're our sister, and nothing you can do is ever going to change that. You're stuck with us for life, woman."

It helped to hear it. Kennedy supposed it was a sign of some kind of growth that she actually believed it. "Thanks. I really needed that."

"Now, about Xander."

Kennedy tensed. "I didn't mean to hurt him. I don't even know how he found out."

"I don't give a damn how he found out. I give a damn about what he did with the information. How dare he come in here and attack you about it? You were the innocent party in all of this. He has no right to be angry with you."

"He feels like I didn't trust him."

"Well boo hoo, poor him. You got put into a situation where you didn't feel like you could trust anybody. Once he calms down a bit, he'll realize that."

"It's not just that. I lied to him. By omission anyway. He thought, all this time, that I left because of him. Because of a fight we had the night I left. He spent all this time blaming himself for running me off, beating himself up for it. He apologized for it that night out at the bluff." Kennedy shook her head. "I barely even remembered it. But that's what he believed and—I let him think it. I let him think it because it seemed safer than telling him anything that would make him ask questions about all this."

"You didn't have a choice. Not then. Surely he'll grow to see that."

"I don't know that it matters, Pru. Right now, he feels like everybody he cares about lied to him. We're all complicit in this in one way or another."

"Don't you be defending him." She shot off the bed and paced from one end of the room to the other. "I have half a mind to go over there and give him a good boot in the ass myself."

The image almost wrangled a ghost of a smile. "Please don't. At this point, Xander just needs to be left alone to work out his own feelings on all of this. If nothing else, it put a stop to us just falling back into a relationship as if nothing ever happened. We aren't the same people we were at eighteen. We shouldn't pretend to be."

Pru crossed her arms with a huff. "Fine. I won't go kick his ass. Even though he totally deserves it. But I wish I could do something."

The truth will set you free. "There is one thing you could do."

"Name it."

"Someone needs to let Maggie and Athena know." Now that the secret was out, she wanted them to know that there'd been a real reason, that she hadn't just been selfish all these years. "But I'm just...not up for rehashing this all over again. Not right now. If you could explain, it would be a big help."

"Of course I'll tell them."

Kennedy could only hope that the knowledge would improve her relationship with the two of them. But, if nothing else, she'd solidified her relationship with Pru, and she felt just a little bit lighter for having told the tale.

She shoved off the bed. "I should get a shower. I'll have to pull out all the stops to make myself look not like I've been sobbing most of the day."

"I've got a few tricks for that. Get your shower. I'll go dig out my cucumber eye gel and the eye drops."

"Thanks." Kennedy began gathering her work clothes, but she stopped as Pru reached the door. "Pru?"

"Yeah?"

"Thanks for believing in me."

Her sister's face softened. "Always."

Xander felt like a stalker. He'd been pulling out of his driveway when he remembered Kennedy was starting work at Elvira's tonight. He considered going by, but nothing he had to say needed an audience. No reason to add further grist to the gossip mill. Plus, the last thing he wanted to do was upset her at work. So he'd waited, driving aimlessly around the county, trying to get his head on straight, to find the right words. Ultimately he'd ended up parked down the street from Elvira's, waiting for closing.

As downtown Eden's Ridge emptied, he slid from the Bronco and walked down to the tavern and around back. No bear tonight. But Joan's SUV—repaired now—was parked beneath the security light with the other employee cars. He kept out of sight, avoiding conversation with anyone else. He didn't know what Kennedy may have told people about them. That people had asked wasn't even a question. He'd made sure of that at the diner, and he wasn't in the mood to explain himself.

Kennedy was almost the last one out.

"Hey."

Her head shot up, along with her hands. Her car key protruded from between the fingers of one fist. Xander approved of the display of caution and kept well back, in case she felt compelled to use it.

"Sorry. Didn't mean to startle you."

Kennedy blew out a breath and dropped her hands. "What are you doing here?"

He shoved his own into his pockets to keep from reaching for her. "Can we talk?"

She hesitated. The harsh security lights illuminated the shadows under her eyes and the faint puffiness that meant she'd been crying.

Xander felt like an even bigger jackass.

"Really talk," he pressed. "As in a conversation where I listen, without having my head up my ass."

A light of something he hoped was interest lit her eyes, but her tone was guarded. "Okay. But somewhere else. Your place? Pru and Ari will be sleeping. I don't want to wake them."

She was expecting a fight. And why shouldn't she after last night? He'd all but come out swinging.

"Sure. Meet you there."

Xander wasn't any clearer on what to say by the time he unlocked his house and let her inside. "Want anything? Something to drink? A snack?" He felt stupid asking, but basic hospitality was too deeply ingrained not to make the offer.

"No." Hands tucked under her arms, she crossed over to the sofa and sat. Her expression was guarded, but he took it as a positive sign that she didn't choose the chair to keep him at a definitive distance. She didn't say a word, just waited with a stiffness bordering on brittle. So he sat beside her, close but not touching. He didn't have the right to touch her.

"I've been trying to figure out how to say this all day."

"Your actions spoke pretty clearly last night." Her quiet words were a slap.

Xander winced. "I'm not proud of that. And I'm not going to make excuses. I'm sorry. I'm so goddamned sorry. For what he did to you. To us. And for my reaction. You're not to blame for any of this. I was an asshole last night. I know how hard it's always been for you to trust people. When I'm in my right mind, I *know* that. I know it was a huge deal that I was one of the few you did trust." God, it killed him to say that in the past tense.

"The fact is, since you came back, it felt like nothing had changed. Not really. It was easy to dive back in because it's what I'd always wanted, deep down. And because nothing really *had* changed for me. But things did change for you. My father terrorized you. To the point that you couldn't risk trusting even the handful of people you'd depended on. And it was a dick thing for me to get angry with you for not trusting me like you'd always trusted me. For not taking into account how what he did affected *you*, not just us. So I'm sorry."

Kennedy watched him with serious green eyes. "It was never about trust. Not now anyway. I didn't want to destroy your family. I know what that's like, and I wouldn't wish it on anyone."

She'd put him first. He could see that now. Maybe he didn't agree with how she'd done it, but she'd avoided the easy road of shifting all the blame to his father. He had to respect the strength of that.

"You didn't deserve any of this."

She dropped her hands to her lap, shoulders slumping with utter exhaustion. "It's not about deserving. And either way, it's done. It's over."

"I hate what he did to us."

"So do I. But we're never getting that time back, no matter how much we wish it or how hard we mourn it. Believe me, I know. I've had considerably longer to do it. This thing has been a shadow on my life for a decade, and God, I just want to move past it."

It was going to take him a while longer to process everything. To make his peace with it and figure out what he wanted to do next with his life, his work. But one thing was crystal clear. "I hope you will. With me. If I haven't fucked it all up."

"You said we were a mistake."

She might as well have punched him in the gut. He wished he could punch himself for saying that.

"Trying to pretend the last ten years didn't happen was the mistake. We're older, more mature, and at least one of us is wiser. But *we've* never been a mistake." He reached out to take her hand and found her fingers cold. "I love you. I've always loved you. I'll never think that's a mistake."

Kennedy shut her eyes, her face twisting as she drew in a long, shuddering breath. Xander's heart gave a simultaneous twist.

He'd ruined everything. The tears glimmering in her lashes were confirmation enough of that.

"I spent years imagining this, you know. How it would go, if you ever found out the truth. You were always furious with your father. You're too honorable a man not to be. But I could never quite envision a scenario where this was a possibility. Where, in the end, you still loved me."

Her hand tightened in his and she opened her eyes. There were tears, yes, and a heartbreaking fragility he knew she'd shown few others. It was a measure of that trust he'd thought he'd lost, and it humbled him.

Cupping her face, he stroked away her tears. "I do. I love you. I'll say it as many times as you need to hear it."

Eyes searching his, she reached out to lay a palm against his cheek. "Show me."

CHAPTER 13

*X*ANDER DREW HER IN, stroking a hand back through her hair before laying his lips on hers. The tenderness in his touch felt like a benediction. He knew all, and he still loved her. The miracle of that had her clinging to him, as if he were a dream that would turn to smoke and disappear. Under the gentle coaxing of his mouth, she began to unwind, releasing the tension and anxiety of the past couple of days. With each, slow degree, her heart began to ache a little less.

His hands slipped beneath her shirt, skimming up her spine. Her skin shivered, then heated as those calloused fingers spanned her shoulders, pulling her to him until she felt surrounded. Until she felt safe. It had been so long since she'd felt truly safe. His mouth moved across her cheek, along the shell of her ear and down the column of her throat. Her head fell back to give him better access. He took his time, trailing languorous kisses up the other side, inching up her shirt as he went. His big hands swept up her rib cage and brushed at the underside of her breasts. They went full and heavy, her nipples taut and aching for his touch.

Kennedy reached back, tugging the shirt up and over her

head. She wished she were wearing something other than the plain cotton bra, something sexy, with satin or lace. But Xander's eyes were dark as his gaze roamed over the newly exposed flesh. They went darker still as she released the catch and drew it off. When he pressed her back, she didn't resist, already anticipating the welcome weight of his big body. But he didn't follow her down, moving instead down the length of her to pull off her shoes. It was such a basic thing, but it did something to her, seeing this powerfully-built man, with her shoe in his hand. Somewhere deep down, something shifted. The wall she'd erected to protect herself when she'd been forced to flee family, friends, and safety began to crumble. And she could let it because he would take care of her.

"Let me see you." Her voice felt thick.

With hooded eyes, Xander tugged off his shirt.

Kennedy's mouth went dry. He'd been in amazing shape back in high school. Football, baseball, and good genes had made sure of that, and she'd more than enjoyed his body. But now...now he was beautiful. His chest was broader, thicker, with a smattering of hair that trailed down the center and disappeared beneath the waistband of jeans that did little to hide an impressive erection. She watched the flex of Xander's biceps as he held himself over her, admiring the curve of muscle, giving in to the temptation to touch. His strength was intoxicating.

He planted one knee on the sofa, between her thighs, as he bent to her chest, pulling one budded nipple into his mouth. She arched up, the growing ache in her center brushing against his leg. It wasn't enough. It wasn't nearly enough to assuage the pulsing need, but she pressed against him, rubbing, seeking in time to his suckling. Switching to the other breast, he reached between them, working open her belt, unfastening the tab of her jeans and drawing the zipper down.

When his hand slid inside her panties, she cried out, bucking into him, needing more of that deliciously possessive touch. Confined by her jeans, the heat of his skin and the pressure of his hand against her core was an exquisite torment.

She wrapped her hand around his wrist and slid the other in to cover his. "More."

Acquiescing to her demand, Xander flexed his fingers, working them slowly between her folds, until he slid one into her wet heat. Kennedy writhed, trying to take him deeper. He added a second finger as he kissed her again, dipping his tongue into her mouth. She welcomed it, welcomed the thrusting rhythm he set. Her hips rose and fell, riding his fingers until her body screamed over that first, brutal edge.

As she came back to herself, Xander was carrying her. To a bed, she hoped, because her legs weren't going to function for anything vertical. He climbed a set of dark stairs, headed down a short hall, and turned into a bedroom. She had a dim impression of big, rustic furniture before he laid her down on the wide, soft mattress. He tugged off her jeans, taking her underwear with them to leave her fully naked. The cool air felt glorious against her heated skin. He followed suit, shedding the last of his clothes and climbing in after her. Then she was lost to sensation, his hard to her soft, as he kissed her again and stoked the flames. She surrendered to him utterly, greedily soaking up everything he gave her, until he forced her to wait, impatient, body vibrating with need, as he rolled away to sheath himself. Then he covered her, his heavier weight pressing her into the mattress.

She welcomed him in the cradle of her hips, arching up to meet him as he slid inside her at last. It was coming home in a way nothing else could be. Love and relief crashed through her, washing away the grief.

This—he—was everything.

Kennedy didn't know she was crying until he kissed away her tears.

"Don't cry, Lark. I've got you."

"Xander." It was all she could manage past the tightness in her throat. So she framed his face in her hands and kissed him, wrapping her legs tighter around his waist.

He began to move, pressing deeper into her, filling all the empty places with his slow, inexorable rhythm. This was more, so much more than what they'd been before. The sweetness of it buoyed her, sweeping her up in a tide of pleasure that left no room for thought, no room for anything but him.

"Look at me," he ordered.

Kennedy forced her eyes open, blinked past the blindness of passion to look into his eyes. The fierce tenderness there rocked her.

"With me." He thrust harder, deeper. "With me," he repeated, and pushed them both over the edge.

Her body pulsed around him as he shuddered through his release, then collapsed like a dead weight on top of her. She couldn't really breathe and didn't care. Xander was breathing hard enough for the both of them, his chest heaving against hers, the warmth of his exhalation tickling her throat. Kennedy slid one hand into the fine hair at his nape, rubbing slow circles as their hearts slowed and she basked in the aftershocks of their lovemaking.

When he shifted to roll off her, she tightened her arms and legs. "Don't you dare. You're perfect exactly where you are."

"Practicalities to take care of," he murmured, pressing a kiss to her cooling skin.

"Damn it."

She felt his smile against her throat.

"I'll be right back."

Kennedy watched his retreating backside for a long moment, admiring the perfection of his ass, before she mustered enough energy to burrow under the covers. He was back less than a minute later, hauling her against him and tangling their legs with a sigh of satisfaction.

"This. This is what we never got to do back in high school."

"I concede it's a definite benefit to being adult lovers." She snuggled in, wrapping tight around him. "God, you feel good. There's nothing like skin on skin."

"I am completely okay with you remaining naked for the duration of your stay. Which, for the record, I hope will be until morning."

Warm and happy, she pressed a kiss against his chest. "I always wanted to wake up with you."

"Who said anything about sleeping?"

Kennedy stopped laughing when she ran her hand down his belly and found him already semi-hard again. "Sleep is entirely overrated."

"We've got a little while yet. Tell me something good."

"Something good?"

His hand strayed lower, tracing lazy patterns on her butt. "We've had a lot of awful the last couple of days. I feel like we need to focus on something good to balance it."

"What we just did felt pretty damned fantastic."

"Just warming up."

She drilled a finger into his ribs. "Cocky."

He laughed and captured her hand. "Confident."

"I'd argue, but I'm clearly the beneficiary in this scenario."

"I'd say the benefits are pretty mutual. But seriously, there has to be something good. With Ari? Or your sisters?"

Kennedy thought of the plan she'd been in the midst of constructing when he'd come over last night. "Well, I don't know if it constitutes something good exactly, but I think I know how to save the house and land."

"Yeah?"

"Partly inspired by you, actually."

He listened intently as she described her idea for turning the house into an inn.

"It doesn't have to be a huge outlay. We have this massive house, with all these bedrooms already. By my calculations, we could have eight guest rooms and still maintain the family space. They'd just need some paint, some spit and polish, and we can outfit most of them with furniture we've already got. The only areas where we might need to make a splurge would be on quality linens. But other than that, application for a business license, and setting up a website to get the word out, we could be up and running in a month or six weeks, to take advantage of the spring tourism season. It would take a little time to build a following, but we'd know by the end of the year whether it's a viable option. And if it is, there are options for expansions."

"That makes so much sense."

She bit her lip. "You don't think it's stupid?" What she really meant was, *You don't think I'm stupid?* It hadn't felt like a dumb idea, while she'd been pulling it together, but sharing it with someone else made it bigger, scarier.

"Absolutely not. This plays perfectly into what the mayor and city council are wanting to do. You've worked in pretty much every area of the hospitality industry, so you're the perfect person to pull the concept together. It's brilliant."

Something in her relaxed. She hadn't realized how much she'd needed to hear someone else back her up. "Well, I don't know about brilliant, but it's workable. And so far it's the only idea on the table."

"What did your sisters say?"

"I haven't told them yet. I've been trying to get everything pulled together and organized so that I can present the whole thing in a formal business plan, like Maggie would do it. None of them expect this kind of thing from me, and I want them to take me seriously."

"If you tell them what you just told me, they can't help but take you seriously. It's a smart move, Kennedy. More, I think it's something your mom would've liked."

He believed in her. No one but Joan had ever believed in her like he did. Was it any wonder she still loved him?

Untangling their legs, she rolled until she straddled him.

Xander grinned. "He's probably got another minute or five recovery time, but I'm sure we can make good use of that span."

Heart full to bursting, Kennedy bent to frame his face between her palms. "I love you, Xander."

He sobered. "Are we okay?"

She considered the question. Moving past the truth of what had happened to split them up didn't mean ignoring it. But as hurtful as his reaction had been...he'd had a lot less time to come to terms with it than she had. She sure as hell wasn't going to hold that against him.

"I think there's probably going to be some adjustment. You were right when you said we're different now than we used to be. But I think we don't just start fresh either. We build on the foundation of the old—something new and stronger. But I want this. I want you."

"Then I'd say we're more than okay."

His hands curved around her ass, and they spent the rest of the night proving his confidence was well justified.

"Back again, huh?" Pru smirked at him as she pulled the door wider to let him into the house, but there was no malice in it.

"Best coffee in town," Xander declared easily, heading straight for the kitchen in what had become a routine over the past week.

"Right, it's the coffee," Pru said. "I'll pretend to believe that."

Kennedy rose from the table when he came into the room, moving straight into his arms. "Morning." Her voice was rough, her body pliant and sleepy against his. Not surprising since she'd been getting up to see him before he went on shift. That meant barely more than five hours of sleep last night. He knew, because he'd followed her home around two. And that just made him think about everything they'd done when she got off her shift at Elvira's. His cock twitched.

Pressing a kiss to Kennedy's temple, he moved to the coffee pot for his alleged reason for being here. It wasn't an entire lie. Sleep had been happening in chunks for the past week. He finished his shift and took a nap until she got off work. They spent a few hours together. Then he got another few hours of shut eye. Kennedy, he knew, would go back to bed for a couple hours after he left for work and Pru took Ari to school. It was an odd schedule, but right now it was working for them.

Xander carried his coffee to the table, sliding onto the long bench beside Kennedy, who snuggled in, her head on his shoulder, eyes drooping.

Ari lifted a brow. "I don't know why you don't just pick somebody's house and stay there."

Kennedy popped an eye open. "Huh?"

"Either spend the night at his place or have Xander come here. It's not like you're fooling anybody sneaking in at two in the morning. You'd both get more sleep that way."

Pru hid a smile in her own coffee. "They didn't fool anybody in high school either."

Heat crept up the back of Xander's neck.

Kennedy appeared unconcerned. "I'll have you know, I am not sneaking. One doesn't have to sneak at twenty-eight. He doesn't stay here because your social worker would frown on it. And I don't stay there because, if I did, I wouldn't make it up in time to see your shining face before you head out to school. Since I work odd hours, I wouldn't get to see you otherwise, except on my days off. So, really, I'm enduring the lack of sleep for you, *hermanita*."

"Your sacrifice is noted and appreciated." Ari forked up more eggs. "Not sure what Maggie will think of it, though."

Kennedy opened the eyes that had drifted shut again. "Maggie?"

"I hadn't had a chance to tell you," Pru said. "She called last night to say she's coming back on the red eye tonight."

"For how long?"

"I don't know yet. A few days anyway. She's supposed to get in tomorrow morning."

At that Kennedy sat up, rubbing the sleep from her eyes. Xander knew she'd been working on her business plan in the limited downtime she wasn't spending with him. He wanted to ask if she'd be ready in time, but she hadn't told Pru yet, and he didn't want to spoil the surprise.

Pru checked the clock. "Finish up your breakfast and get your teeth brushed, kiddo. Time to head to school."

Ari finished shoveling in her breakfast and sprinted from the room.

"Out of the mouths of babes, huh?" Pru asked.

"I'm not sure how I feel about her being that astute," Xander admitted.

"A fencepost would know what's going on with you two. But seriously, I am happy for you. Especially so after finding out about—well."

Xander scowled.

Kennedy squeezed his arm, setting her chin on his shoulder. "It's done. Let it go."

"I've got to see him today. We've got a department briefing I can't miss."

"Frankly, I'm impressed you managed to avoid him for this long. Do you know what you're going to say?"

"I've already said what I'm going to say on the matter." Xander was more concerned with what his father might say, what additional justification he might attempt to offer. If Buck honestly tried to say he'd been in the right, Xander wasn't sure he could be held responsible for his response.

"Then, for now, go in, do the job, get out."

She made it sound so easy. But it was going to take him a whole lot longer to come to terms with his father's betrayal.

Ari came back into the kitchen. "Ready. If we go now, they might have time to canoodle before Xander has to leave for work."

Kennedy hurled a piece of toast at her. "You're not too old to ground, you know."

"Do you even know what canoodling is?" Xander asked.

"I assume it involves sucking face."

"Ooookay." Pru spun Ari around and shoved her toward the door. "We're going. Xander, have a good day. Kennedy, I'll probably see you before you leave for work. My client schedule is on the desk."

"Make good choices!" Ari called cheerfully from the foyer.

Kennedy snorted and the front door shut behind them.

"Well, I guess we're busted," Xander said. "By a thirteen year old, no less."

"I'm a lot less bothered by that than the fact that apparently my mother was aware of our love life."

Xander froze in utter horror as he imagined Joan Reynolds crossing her arms, giving him The Eyebrow, and asking exactly what his intentions were toward her daughter. "Oh God."

"She—"

He held up a hand. "No, stop. Leave me with whatever delusions I have left. If people know what we did in that hay loft, I don't wanna know about it."

"Fair enough."

"She's gonna be a real ball buster. Ari, I mean."

"She is. And she's going to have to be hella inventive to get away with anything because, between the four of us, and everyone else who came through here, we've seen or done pretty much everything."

Xander rose and took his empty coffee cup to the sink. "Are you ready for Maggie to know about your plan for the inn?"

"No, but it seems I've got about twenty-four hours to get there. Fortunately, that set of test bedding I wanted came in yesterday. I managed to sneak it upstairs, while Pru was with a client. Can I get you to help me shove furniture to the middle of the room before you head out?"

He'd rather test the bedding. "My muscles are yours to command." He pulled her into his arms, then ran his hands down over her ass.

Kennedy pursed her lips. "We don't have time for that level of canoodling. More's the pity. But I'll see you when I get off tonight. Help me do this, then go to work. Protect and serve. Don't kill your dad. They don't offer sufficient conjugal visits in prison."

Because he knew she was trying to lighten the mood, he worked up a smile. "There's a motivation."

She rose on her toes and brushed her lips over his in a lingering kiss that had him wishing he could set his own hours.

"Tonight," he breathed.

"Tonight."

Xander had himself under control by the time he made it to the station. He'd spent minimal time there the past week, coming in after hours to complete reports, update files. The moment he walked in, everybody stopped talking.

"Morning."

Clyde Parker, the other Stone County Deputy, opened his mouth, but before he could blurt out whatever fool thing had crossed his mind, Leanne dug an elbow into his gut.

"Hi, Xander," she said.

Jarvis nodded. "Mornin'."

"We're, um, just about ready to start the briefing." Essie chewed her lip, which left a hot pink smudge on her teeth.

Nobody knew how to act. And why should they? Chances were this place was on the verge of World War III.

Xander crossed over to his desk, depositing his service weapon in the lock box in the bottom drawer. No reason to walk in there armed. This was a professional meeting.

The door to his father's office opened, and Buck called a gruff, "Let's get this thing started."

Everybody filed in. Xander took a position on the far side of the office, well out of Buck's reach. Not that he expected the old man to take a swing at him, but he wanted to remove temptation. His dad gave him a long look, face inscrutable, before launching into the briefing. Xander listened, took notes as necessary. He answered questions asked of him and generally maintained a professional demeanor for the duration of the meeting. It was a reasonable facsimile of a normal day.

Every single person in the room knew it wasn't a normal day.

Xander had no idea what details Essie and Leanne may have shared with the others. They all gossiped like a bunch of teenage girls most of the time, so he was willing to bet everything that was on file and at least some of Essie's personal recollections. Certainly they all knew he'd stormed out to confront his father and that he'd been avoiding Buck ever since.

But the détente couldn't last.

As the meeting reached its natural conclusion, Buck dismissed everybody. "Xander, I need to talk to you about the county fair. The mayor's wanting to change the parade route this year."

It was a weak excuse and everyone knew it, but Xander knew he couldn't put this off forever. So he stayed put as his coworkers left the office. Essie was the last one out. The door shut behind her with a quiet click that might as well have been the hammer of a gun.

"The fair's not until June," Xander said.

"I don't give a rat's ass about the fair."

"I don't give a rat's ass what you have to say."

"How the hell am I supposed to apologize if you keep avoiding me?"

"Apologize? Really? You think you can fix this with an apology?"

"It'd be a start."

"Drop in the bucket, Dad. Do you even know what you're apologizing for? Or is it just that you're sorry you got caught?" A new thought occurred to him. "You're up for re-election this year. Imagine what your constituents would have to say about such a flagrant abuse of power."

Buck went pale. "It was a mistake."

"A mistake? Copying down an address wrong from a driver's license is a mistake. Transposing the numbers for clocked speed on a ticket is a mistake. Failing to properly mirandize a suspect in custody and emotionally blackmailing her for personal reasons is a gross misuse of the badge. Do you know what you did to her? Because it wasn't just sending her away from me. You gave her an impossible choice. You damaged her relationship with her sisters, with her mother. She barely got to see Joan over the past decade because you made her too scared to ever come home. And now Joan's dead and she can't ever get that relationship back."

"She didn't have to leave the country—"

"Don't you dare. She left because if she'd been anywhere stateside, I would've found her. She left because you made her think that if she so much as breathed wrong, you'd destroy her relationship with her family and arrest her on a felony. If anybody deserves an apology and restitution, it's Kennedy. I hope you do try. You owe her that. And I hope she spits in your face. Because you deserve that. See, I've clarified for her all the lies you told, all the little manipulations of the truth. She's not running scared anymore. She's here to stay. With me. So you'd best get used to it."

"Xander, I—"

"Let me make one thing perfectly clear. I'll do the job, but every shred of respect I have for you as a father and as Sheriff is gone. From this day forward, you're dead to me."

Without another word, Xander strode out.

CHAPTER 14

KENNEDY WAS A LOT less confident about her plan than she'd let Xander believe. She wasn't finished with the formalized proposal for the business. The necessary number crunching had taken a backseat to work and spending time with him. Given the time constraints, she didn't think she'd be able to pull all of it together by tomorrow morning, especially since she had to work tonight to help cover the Friday night rush. But if a picture was worth a thousand words, hopefully a fully set up room would be worth more. She sent a quick series of texts to Denver, to see if she could go in late. She had a busy day ahead of her.

Figuring out how to buy paint and supplies and sneak them into the house without Pru knowing made Kennedy feel a little bit like a spy. She'd memorized Pru's whole client schedule for the day and deliberately picked one of the third floor rooms to avoid likelihood of discovery. With a hastily scrawled note left on the kitchen counter, she told Pru she was running a quick errand, then catching up on sleep. God bless her soft-hearted sister. Pru would believe it and keep quiet and out of the way.

She thought of Xander on the drive into town. He'd been avoiding his father for more than week, and Kennedy was worried about how this would go. He wasn't going to just forgive and forget. She knew there'd been one blow up already before he'd come to her about it, but there'd been no resolution. The fact was, they worked together and had for the better part of a decade. So either they figured some way to work things out or one of them left the job. Kennedy couldn't see any middle ground. As they *were* law enforcement in Stone County, it wasn't like there was really another option here. Xander could leave—take a job elsewhere. But he wouldn't go without her, and she wouldn't go because of Ari. She'd promised. Which put them between as much a rock and a hard place as the original devil's choice Buck had given her.

Kennedy made it back to the house while Pru was with her first client of the day. She hustled upstairs with her purchases. In less than an hour, she had all the trim taped off and had poured the first glug of paint into the tray. She'd chosen a palette of soft grays and misty greens in shades that reminded her of the mountains she so loved. The dove gray walls would bring the outside in, especially on misty mornings with the sun shining through the dormer window, and the bedding she'd bought would, hopefully, make guests feel like they were napping in a mountain glen.

Her phone dinged with a text. Xander to say how the briefing went? She checked the display. But it was her boss, granting permission for her to come in late. She sent off a quick thank you, then texted Xander because she was worried about him.

His reply came back almost immediately. **It's done.**

It's done? What the hell does that mean?

But text wasn't the way to get into it. They'd talk later. She had way too much to get done first.

Kennedy: **Going into work late tonight. Can you swing by after five to help shove this furniture back in place?**

Xander: **Sure. Good luck.**

Dipping in the roller, Kennedy got to work.

Hours later, the door swung open. Crouched down on the floor painting trim, Kennedy couldn't hold in the squeak of surprise. Excuses jumbled in her mind, but it was Ari, not Pru.

"Wow! Who knew paint would make such a difference?"

"Quiet!" Kennedy hissed. "Come in and shut the door if you're coming."

Ari did as asked. "So you're getting ready to show Maggie the idea for the inn?"

"That's the plan. If I can get ready in time. The walls are pretty much dry, but the trim will take until much later. I think, if we're careful, we can get the furniture back in place without messing anything up, though."

The girl eyed the massive armoire. "I'm not sure we can move that carefully. Or quietly."

"Xander's coming back by to help me shift things around before I leave for work."

"Oh, Xander." She drew his name out in that knowing, sing-song tone only teenage girls could pull off.

Kennedy fixed her with a flat stare.

Unperturbed, Ari just grinned. "So what's the deal with you two?"

"The deal is that I need help finishing this trim. If you're going to interrupt me, you're going to work."

She grabbed a brush and plopped down on the floor beside the paint bucket.

"Don't drip," Kennedy cautioned.

"I won't. So, you and Xander. Tell me the story."

"There's not much to tell." There was so much to tell, but much of it wasn't appropriate for teenage ears. "We used to be together back in high school. Now that I'm back, we've got a second chance, and we're taking it."

"Oh no, that's not enough payoff for painting. Tell me about you back in high school."

This Kennedy could talk about. She'd spent so long focused on the sadness and regret that this—getting to share all the good memories she had with Xander and remember how happy they'd been—it felt like a gift. "He was the star running back for the football team." They painted and she talked, telling Ari about their love story—leaving out the steamier bits. Kennedy had no idea if Ari had a boy she liked, but no reason to give her ideas. And it was good to remember all those early days and how in love they'd been.

"Joan kept pictures of the two of you."

"Did she?" Those hadn't been in the travel scrapbooks. She'd have to go hunt them up later.

"It was obvious you two were nuts about each other."

"We were." *Still are.*

"If you loved him so much, why did you leave?"

Should've known she wouldn't be satisfied with only part of the story. Dragging her brush along the last section of trim, Kennedy tried to decide what to tell her. It would be easy to blame Buck. And certainly he'd been the primary reason. But what she'd told Xander about feeling unworthy of the family hadn't been a lie. If she hadn't felt that, hadn't been so terrified of being thrown away, she wouldn't have been so susceptible to his father's emotional blackmail. And given Ari's tenuous position in the family, it was the part Kennedy most wanted to share.

"A lot of complicated reasons. Some of which I'm just not going to get into. But some of it was that I was really messed up. My parents threw me away. I could make excuses for them, but in the end, that was the reality. Joan wasn't my first foster placement. I went through several before I ended up here, and I saw plenty of turnover in the system of other foster kids hitting eighteen and just getting dumped. Even after I came here, even after Mom adopted me, that stuck with me. And there was a part of me that never really felt like I belonged. A part that expected that I'd be booted out when I hit eighteen. So I was determined to go before anybody else had a chance to throw me away." Before anyone could give Joan reason to.

She set her brush aside and pivoted to face Ari. The girl was frowning hard, a line marring the skin between her brows.

"I was wrong. It took me a long time to accept that. I was always a part of this family and nothing I ever did or said could ever have changed that. I say all this because you remind me so much of me. I know you're worried about what's going to happen to you. I know we don't have the same legal protections we'd have if the adoption had gone through before Mom died. But whatever the hell it says on paper, you are part of this family. If you learned nothing else from your time with Joan, you should have learned that the family you make is a helluva lot stronger than the one you're born into. You're ours, and all of us are going to fight for you."

Ari swiped an arm over glimmering eyes. "I've never met anybody like y'all."

"Fellow misfits, one and all." She wrapped her arms around the younger girl. "Now come on and help me finish this trim so we can go pick out lamps and accessories."

"CAREFUL, careful. Don't let it touch the wall. The trim isn't quite dry yet." Under normal circumstances, Kennedy would have waited until tomorrow, but there simply wasn't time. She bit her lip as Xander muscled the bed back another few inches. "There! That's it!" She clapped her hands and did a little happy dance, complete with a hip bump for Ari.

The corner of Xander's mouth turned up at that. "Anything else?"

He was trying to cover up his mood, but Kennedy knew him

and knew that he was struggling with whatever had happened with his father.

"It still needs to be dressed and staged, but I so don't have time to do all that before I go to work." She wished she were off work entirely for the night so she could finish and so they could finally talk about his dad and about the email she'd gotten from Elena this afternoon about the book proposal. But beggars couldn't be choosers. She was grateful Denver had given her as much time as he had.

Xander looked around at the rearranged furniture, the freshly painted walls and trim. "I can't believe you got all this done today."

"I helped!" Ari announced.

"You did, indeed." Kennedy had enjoyed the hell out of spending time with the girl. "And you can help some more by running down to my room and hauling up the bedding I've got stashed there. Then it will be here and ready to go in the morning, and I don't have to worry about sneaking it past anybody to maintain the surprise."

"I can make the bed. Then you don't have to."

Oh, this kid. She'd embraced the idea and run with it, displaying a level of enthusiasm only teenagers could manage. Kennedy reached out to squeeze Ari's shoulder. "That'd be awesome.

"Okay. I'll walk really loud when I come back, so you'll know when to stop making out."

Xander choked on a half laugh as she left the room. "We're never going to hear the end of this, are we?"

Given all the questions she'd asked about them today, Kennedy was banking on that being the literal truth. "She's at an age where kissing is fascinating."

He scowled. "So long as she's just thinking and not doing."

Kennedy looped her arms behind his neck and grinned up at him. "Are you going all protective big brother?"

"Someone has to."

"That's adorable."

"That's practical. I used to be a thirteen year old boy. They're more fascinated with boobs. Maybe I should teach her some self-defense."

"Never a bad thing," Kennedy agreed. "Though I am reasonably sure she thinks the boys her age are morons."

"The ones older than her are even worse. Self-defense," he decided. "I'll find some time to squeeze it in."

"You're so cute." She rose on her toes and pressed her lips to his.

She meant it as a quick peck, but Xander wrapped his arms around her, fitting her body against his. He didn't devour her, though she could feel the edge of that temptation simmering between them. He seemed to be searching out some sweetness. So she pushed thoughts of Buck, of the inn, of the book from her mind and poured every ounce of comfort she could into the kiss.

The sound of the door opening had Xander reluctantly lifting his head. "I thought you were gonna walk loud," he complained.

"When have I ever walked loud?"

Kennedy went rigid. *No!*

Maggie stood framed in the doorway, a tired smile on her face. "So that's on again, is it? Glad to see some good news."

Behind her Ari mimed *Sorry!*

Kennedy disentangled herself, mind already spinning in search of an explanation for the room. "We weren't expecting you until the morning."

"I caught an earlier flight." Maggie shoved the door open wider. The moment she stepped inside, her face went pale. "What have you done?"

Kennedy's nerves went taut at the immediate tone of disapproval. "I'm not finished yet. I wanted to have everything set up before I showed you." This was all wrong. Incomplete. This wasn't how she'd wanted to present the concept to her sister.

Xander gave her a supportive squeeze.

Maggie turned a circle, taking in the freshly painted walls and trim. "You've destroyed it."

Irritation or exasperation she'd expected. But this kind of accusation left her stunned and confused. "I...what? It's just paint. I was freshening everything up. I know the gray isn't the warmest tone, but once you see it with the bedding, you'll get the full effect."

Maggie looked like she was ready to vomit. One arm wrapped across her middle, the other hand covered her mouth.

Kennedy rushed on, trying to find some way to salvage this train wreck. "If you hate the color that much, we can paint again. It's not a big deal."

"Not a big deal," Maggie repeated, voice trembling. "Oh you have no idea how big a deal this is."

This was bad. So. Very. Bad.

Pru appeared in the doorway. "Look who showed up early!" Her cheerful smile faded as she registered the tension. "What's going on?" She came into the room and saw for herself. "Oh. Oh dear."

"How could you do this?" Maggie demanded.

Okay maybe Kennedy hadn't expected a double pompom yay reaction to her makeover, but she certainly hadn't expected this. "Do what? I deliberately picked one of the rooms that wasn't the family space."

Xander's phone rang, slicing through the tension before he reached into his pocket to silence it. "Why don't we all take this down a few notches?"

Maggie ignored him, her hands curling into fists. "Not the family space? Have you been gone so long that you've forgotten how we define family here? This was Lauren's room. Susan's. Porter's. Alex's. They were all family."

What the hell was this about? "I never said they weren't. But no one's been up here in ages. I don't understand what I've done wrong."

"Of course you don't. Because you didn't ask. You didn't discuss it with anybody. You just *did it.* You're always just doing what you want without taking anybody else into account. You haven't been here in *years,* so how could you possibly make a decision like this without consulting us?" Maggie's voice had risen to a shout.

"Now hold on a damn minute!"

Kennedy shot out a hand as Xander started to step in front of her. She'd done this, whatever it was. She'd face it herself. But most of the blood had drained out of her face, and she was shaky and cold. None of this was going how she'd planned. "I was just trying to help." She hated that her voice came out small, almost childlike.

"Help? How does this help anything?" Maggie demanded.

"I was working on an idea that could save the house without the trust."

Maggie threw up her hands and turned an angry circle, glaring at the walls as if she could incinerate the changes with a look. "Really, Kennedy?"

Kennedy's shoulders slumped and she could actually feel her confidence evaporating. This was a mistake. A disaster, though she couldn't understand why. And it didn't matter that she wasn't finished, didn't matter that she'd done the work and the plan made sense. Maggie would never hear her now.

But before she could reply, Ari was stepping between them, arms folded across her thin chest, chin jutting. "It's a good idea."

"You were in on this?" Maggie managed a slightly calmer tone with the child.

"Yeah. We were going to surprise you all once everything was finished."

"Surprise me." Maggie rubbed a hand over her eyes.

"I'm sure Kennedy meant well," Pru interjected. "She didn't know it was going to be the nursery."

The nursery? Realization slammed into Kennedy. This room had been intended as the nursery for Maggie's baby. Might very well have been one of the last memories she'd had attached to that time.

Oh. Oh shit. What have I done?

"The road to hell is paved with good intentions," Maggie bit out.

"That's *enough*," Xander snapped. His phone began to ring again.

"Maybe you should get that instead of sticking your nose in family business," Maggie said.

Xander stepped up to Maggie, toe-to-toe. "Family business does not give you the right to abuse your sister. It doesn't give you the right to treat her as an outsider or a screw up. She's none of those things. But you wouldn't know that, would you? Because you didn't bother to ask. You've just made assumptions."

Kennedy hunched her shoulders, wishing she could curl up into a ball and hide from all the hard words and hateful tones.

Someone's text notification went off.

"And you didn't the last ten years?" Maggie fired back.

"I *asked* as soon as I had the chance."

Kennedy couldn't take it anymore. She laid a hand on his shoulder. "Xander, don't."

"The hell I won't. I'm not going to stand by and let her attack you. You're mine and they damned well better get used to the fact that you don't stand alone anymore."

"Oh my God. Xander."

None of them even spared Pru a glance.

"She's been working her ass off for the last two weeks trying to fix someone else's mess and you *will* give her the courtesy of listening to her plan."

Maggie's cool eyes turned hot.

"Xander!" The edge of panic in Pru's voice had them all turning toward her.

"What?" he growled.

"I just got a text from your mom. Your father's had a heart attack."

CHAPTER 15

*X*ANDER CALLED HIS MOTHER back, somehow managing to keep his voice calm and even, despite the fact that every cell in his body was dialed to disbelief or panic. He tried to focus on what she was saying but could barely hear past the roaring in his ears. Was this what it had been like for Kennedy when Pru called about Joan? Instinctively, he reached for her, curling trembling fingers around hers.

Realizing his mom had stopped talking, he forced himself to speak. "I'll meet you there." He'd gotten the location of the hospital, at least.

"Hurry."

He hung up the phone, then just stared at the blank screen, the last words he'd spoken to his father echoing through his brain.

From this day forward, you're dead to me.

What had he done?

"Xander?" Kennedy's soft voice was as much a reminder of support as a question.

Feeling utterly lost, he lifted his head to look at her. "I... He's been rushed to the hospital in Johnson City."

"Then let's go."

"I..." Xander closed his eyes, at war with himself. He was still so fucking *angry*. And his father might be dying.

Kennedy closed the distance between them, pulling him into a tight embrace. He wrapped his arms around her, burying his face in her hair, beyond grateful that she was here.

"It doesn't matter how angry you are with him right now. If you don't go, you'll regret it."

His shuddering inhale shook them both. "Okay." This was a disaster. He was trained to handle disasters. He could do this. He stepped back. "Okay."

"Give me your keys." Kennedy held out a hand.

"I'm in the cruiser. You can't legally drive it."

"Then we'll take Joan's Jeep. You're in no shape to drive."

He didn't argue.

Her sisters trailed them down the stairs.

"Keep us updated," Pru said. "And let us know what we can do."

Kennedy said something he didn't hear. Then they were in the Jeep, flying out of town. She didn't pressure him to speak on the half-hour drive, and he was grateful. He didn't think he could process any of this yet. But he held tight to her hand because she was his lifeline.

They found his mother in the waiting room. Marilyn leapt up at the sight of him. "Xander!" Then her gaze slid to Kennedy and her step faltered.

The idea of not bringing Kennedy had never even crossed his mind, but at that little hitch, Xander began to wonder if her being here was the right thing after all. She'd come to support him, but what kind of toll would this take on her?

He pulled his mother in for a tight hug. "What's going on?"

"They've rushed him in for emergency surgery." Her pretty face was streaked with tears. "Beyond that, I don't know."

Xander held her by the elbows, struggling to keep his composure. "What happened?"

Marilyn's gaze strayed to Kennedy. Just a quick, involuntary glance, but Xander saw it. "His conscience caught up with him."

No, not his conscience. Xander. This was because of him, because he'd gone to war for her, trying to make his father pay for his wrongs. It seemed he'd done too good a job.

Marilyn turned to face Kennedy, fresh distress written across her features. "Kennedy, what he did—"

"Don't." Kennedy's tone was gentle. "That's not what's important right now."

That she could set all that aside after what his father had done... She was a better person than he was, and he felt humbled that she was with him.

His mother's lips trembled. She reached out to take Kennedy's hand. "Thank you for coming."

The waiting was excruciating. Kennedy made an effort to distract them both for a few hours with a continuous string of stories from her travels. She brought them bad coffee, tried to get them both to eat something. And the clock kept ticking. Eventually, sometime after the four-hour mark, his mother fell asleep, slumped in one of the waiting room chairs. A kind nurse brought a pillow and blanket. Xander paced to the window as Kennedy used them to make her as comfortable as possible. Guilt and dread churned in his gut. Why the hell hadn't the doctors come to tell them anything?

Kennedy joined him at the window, looking out into the night. "Your mom's asleep finally. How you holding up?"

A muscle ticked in his jaw. He didn't look at her, couldn't, as he admitted, "This is all my fault."

"Pretty sure you can't be responsible for the condition of your dad's heart." Her words were matter-of-fact, and under any other circumstances, maybe they'd have helped.

"I'm sure as hell responsible for saying the things that pushed him over the edge."

Sliding an arm around his waist, she said, "Tell me."

Maybe it would help to confess it like a sin in church. He dropped his head forward, pressing his brow to the cool glass. "After the meeting, he tried to apologize. As if an apology would make up for what he did. I told him as much. Dressed him down for his behavior and threatened to make the whole thing public so he'd never get re-elected. I told him he'd lost all my respect, as a sheriff and as a father. And I—" His voice broke. "I said he was dead to me."

"Oh, Xander." Kennedy turned into him.

He didn't deserve the comfort, but he held on anyway because she was the only thing keeping him from flying apart. "I knew he didn't look quite right, but I just thought, well, that's what he looked like when I finally defied him. And I just walked out."

"You were angry."

That was no excuse. "I should've realized—"

"Did your dad have a known heart condition?"

Xander tried to think. "I—not that I'm aware of."

"Then you couldn't have known," she insisted. "You were angry and it was your right to be so, your right to express it. You have too strong a sense of justice not to want consequences for what he did."

"But I didn't mean this." No matter how angry he was, he'd never have wished this.

"Of course not. And you didn't do this. This is not on you."

"But—"

"Listen. I came back. I was the reminder of when he broke the rules. Did something awful. Does that make any of this is my fault?"

He didn't hesitate. "Absolutely not."

"Okay then." She stroked his cheek. "I admit the timing is

awful, but we didn't do this. It is a thing that happened. It's no one's fault."

What she said made sense, but it didn't combat his biggest fear. "But...what if he dies? What if he dies, and that's the last thing I ever said to him?" He'd never forgive himself.

"Don't think about that. You need to be putting out positive energy. He's going to come through this. He's going to get better. You're going to get to talk to him again. You're going to get the chance to forgive him."

The anger flared anew amid the maelstrom of other emotions. Even with his father possibly dying, he hadn't let go of that. "Forgive him? After what he did to you? To us?"

Kennedy framed his face in her hands. "And we're together despite it. We're together, Xander, despite everything. Yes, he did a terrible thing, but that doesn't negate the fact that he's your father and he's still basically a good man. The forgiveness isn't really for him. It's for you. Because as long as you hang on to that anger, it's going to poison you from the inside out. It's going to eat away at you."

He searched her face. "Can you forgive him?"

She didn't answer immediately, clearly giving the question some serious thought. Her whole life had changed because of him. She'd lost time with her mother that she'd never get a chance to make up. Her relationships with her sisters were rocky, at best. All that was on Buck. It was a lot to forgive.

At length, her expression smoothed out. "I think I can. Because, in the end, he's the one who has to live with what he did. I don't. Not anymore."

"Mr. Kincaid?"

They both turned as a white coated woman approached.

"Your father's out of surgery."

"He's awake."

Marilyn shot out of the chair. "Can we see him?"

"One at a time, and only for a little while," the nurse cautioned.

"You go in first," Xander urged.

With a quick nod, Mom disappeared into the room across the hall.

Xander dropped his head to Kennedy's shoulder. "Thank God."

She ran gentle fingers through his hair. "I told you it would be okay. Power of positive thinking."

"You'll have to give me lessons in that."

His father was awake. He'd survived a massive heart attack and double bypass surgery. The old bastard was tough. According to the doctors, he should make a full recovery. Relief left Xander feeling weak and exhausted. Or maybe that was the fact that he'd been up for somewhere around twenty-eight hours now.

"I'm glad you're here."

Kennedy leaned her head against his. "Wouldn't be anywhere else."

They sat like that for several minutes. Xander thought about what she'd said earlier. Could he really forgive his father for his own sake? He didn't know. Probably wouldn't until he saw him again.

The door opened and Mom slipped out. "He looks rough, but he's going to be okay. He wants to see you."

Kennedy squeezed his hand. "Say what you need to say."

It would be awesome if he knew what that was.

With a bracing breath, he went inside.

His father looked smaller somehow against the crisp white sheets. His face was sickly gray and seemed ten years older than yesterday morning. But the steady, incessant beep of the heart monitor was a clear reminder that he was still kicking. Although it seemed he'd fallen back asleep.

Buck's eyes opened. "Got things to say to you." Even his voice sounded weaker, his words slurring. It freaked Xander out. His father had never been anything but hale and hearty.

"You shouldn't talk, Dad. You need to rest."

"I need to talk and you need to listen. If nearly dying didn't grant me that right, then I don't know what can."

At the brash reminder of his brush with death, Xander's own heart squeezed. "Look, Dad, I said some things yesterday—"

"You didn't say anything that wasn't warranted. Now shut up and listen, boy."

With no other choice, Xander sat in the lone chair and shut up."

"I've been a cop for going on forty years. I devoted my life to serving our community and keeping it safe. And somehow that night, I pushed all that aside."

Xander didn't need to ask which night.

"I can't tell you what was in my head. I don't know. It was late, and I saw an opportunity, and I acted on it. I used scare tactics on that girl that I normally reserved for hardened criminals, and I strong armed her into leaving town and walking away from you. I made threats I'd never have carried out, pressed on every weak spot I knew she had. I'm not proud of that. And I regretted it within a week when I saw what I'd done to you. But I convinced myself that it was for the best. That if she was really yours, she'd come back, and if she wasn't, well, it wasn't meant to be. When she didn't come back, I figured you'd eventually get over it and move on. You didn't. She stayed gone, and I never had a chance to fix it."

It turned out Xander's anger wasn't entirely extinguished. The simmer and bubble of it had him clenching his fists, though he kept his voice level. "You could've gotten her contact information from Joan or Pru. Let her know it was all a lie."

"Not without good reason. Not without admitting to what I'd done. And I—I was too much a coward for that. What I did to

Kennedy is my greatest shame. And I'm sorry for it. I know that's not worth jack shit. But maybe this will be." Buck struggled to sit up in bed, cursing when he couldn't. "Damn it, I'm not saying this while I'm flat on my back."

"Wait just a minute." Xander helped him find the remote that lifted the head of the bed and adjusted it so he was a bit more upright.

"I spent the afternoon drafting my letter of resignation."

Xander's mouth fell open. "You did what?"

"You were right. My behavior was a disgrace to the badge. I'm not the kind of man Stone County would want as its Sheriff."

"Dad." Never in a million years would he have expected this.

"The letter's in the top drawer of my desk. I want you to go find it. Read it."

"Why?"

"Because I wanted you to know I was planning on turning it in before this shit." He waved a weak hand toward the IV and other assorted tubes and wires. "Doctor tells me I gotta retire anyway unless I wanna end up in the ground sooner rather than later. That'd really piss your mama off. I been promising her for twenty years that we could do some traveling when I retired."

Xander felt his lips twitch. "I'll find it. What do you want me to do with it after?"

"That's up to you. I'd rather publicly retire for health reasons, if only to save your mother from the gossip and backlash the other would bring. But that'll be your call. Either way, I think you should replace me. You've got more honor and integrity in your little finger than anybody else I know. And I've known some fine men and women. You deserve the job."

Him as Sheriff? Xander had never even considered it. He'd just kind of assumed his father would live forever. But he found he didn't hate the idea. Did he really want to run for Sheriff? That was not something to ponder on this little sleep. "I expect that'll be up to the people of Stone County."

"Expect it will. Your girl still here? Marilyn said she came."

Xander tensed. "She's in the hall."

"Bring her in. Please."

"If you upset her—" Xander let the threat hang between them.

"Not trying to upset anybody. I'm just trying to make amends."

When Xander got back to the ICU waiting room, Kennedy rose from her seat beside his mother. "You okay?"

"Working on it. He wants to see you." At the look of outright shock, Xander took her hands. "You don't have to if you don't want to."

"No, it's fine." Squaring her shoulders, she followed him back inside.

From the bed, Buck watched them, eyes skimming over their linked hands.

"How are you feeling, Sheriff?"

"Like I got hit by a Mack truck. But they tell me I'll live."

"That's good. You gave everybody a scare."

How could she stand here and have a conversation with his father, as if they didn't have all this toxic shit between them?

"Seems I'm right good at that," Buck said. His head drooped a bit, but the old man strained to keep eye contact with Kennedy. "I want to apologize to you. I was wrong. Completely. I know that's not worth anything at this late date, and nothing I can say or do will make up for what I took from you both. But right now apologies and regrets are all I've got."

Kennedy angled her head in acknowledgment. "I appreciate that. And, for what it's worth, I forgive you."

Buck's head dipped, his gaze dropping to somewhere around his toes. "I don't deserve that."

"That's the thing about forgiveness. It's not something you earn. It has to be given freely or it's not really forgiveness at all."

God, this woman. She had more compassion and wisdom in her little finger than most people learned in a lifetime. That she could stand here and honestly mean everything she'd just said—and Xander had no doubt she meant it—left him absolutely in awe and so proud of her, his chest felt fit to burst.

"You're a far better person than I ever gave you credit for."

Kennedy offered a rueful smile. "I get that a lot."

Xander drew her into his side and pressed a kiss to her temple. This woman would never cease to amaze him. "For what it's worth, I'm not quite there yet. But I'm working on it."

"Better than I can expect," his father said equably.

They lapsed into a weighted silence.

"So…you two are back together, then."

"Yep," Xander answered.

Buck nodded, something lightening in his face. "I reckon that means we've gotta find a way to co-exist." He looked to Kennedy, flummoxed. "How do we do that?"

"You love your son." She looked up at Xander. "So do I. Why don't we start there?"

CHAPTER 16

"ARE YOU SURE IT'S okay if I sleep here?"

Kennedy was pretty sure if she didn't steer him toward a bed in the next five minutes, Xander would collapse on the nearest horizontal surface. "It's fine. Go on up to my room. I'll be up in a little bit after I give everybody the update."

He stroked a thumb across her cheek. "Don't be long."

She found a smile for him and nudged him toward the stairs. He trudged up, each step seeming to take twice as long as it should have. Kennedy hoped he managed to get his shoes off before he tumbled into bed.

Hearing voices, she headed for the kitchen.

Her sisters looked up from the table when she came into the room.

"Kennedy! You're back." Ari leapt up and came to hug her.

Pru followed suit. "What can I get you? Coffee? Food?"

"Nothing. I'm loaded up on crappy hospital food and coffee. I'm about to go pass out. And just so you know, Xander is sleeping here. He's had a really rough couple of days. If anybody has a problem with that, I'll sleep in a different bed, but he doesn't need to be alone."

"Of course it's fine. How's Buck?" Pru asked.

"He's a tough son of a bitch. Double bypass surgery. But they say he's going to be okay."

"Gotta say, a massive heart attack seems like karmic payback to me." Athena's disembodied voice came from the iPad on the table. "Like the guilt finally got to him for what he did to you."

Apparently Kennedy had arrived home in the middle of a family meeting. One excluding her. Again.

"I'd hate to think that," she said.

"You're nicer than I am. I have a much finer-tuned sense of vengeance."

Maggie rose from the other end of the table. "Listen, Kennedy, about last night—"

Kennedy held up a hand. "Can you not? If you want to yell at me some more, fine, but it's going to wait until I've had some sleep. I've been up for thirty hours, and I'm feeling mean."

Maggie's cheeks flushed. "I don't want to yell at you. I want to talk to you. Which is what I *should* have done in the first place. I'm sorry."

The sudden turnaround had Kennedy's head spinning. Or maybe that was the lack of sleep. "Okay?"

"You want to turn the house into an inn." It wasn't a question.

Kennedy realized that all her notes were spread out over the kitchen table. "Where did you get those?" It was a stupid question. From her room, obviously. That was where she'd stashed them.

"Ari pulled them out after you left last night," Pru explained.

Kennedy wished she hadn't done that. Wished she'd had the chance to organize everything the way she'd wanted. But wishing something didn't make it true. So she mustered up a smile of thanks for the girl, who'd only been trying to help.

Maggie laid a hand on the open binder. "You've put a lot of work into this."

That sounded like the kind of statement you made when you

weren't impressed with the end results but needed to find something positive to say, and it put Kennedy's back up. "I'm not finished with it."

"If you did this much in just a week, I'd love to see what you could do with more time."

Kennedy squinted at Maggie, trying to decide if she was being punked. Or maybe she'd really fallen asleep, and she was still curled up in a chair at the hospital. "You would?"

"The design layouts for each room, the costs and time projections for getting each one ready for guests, the expected costs per guest with the anticipated revenue generated—that's all very well done. The phased rollout and expansion options based on success rate is brilliant. And the website mock up...Kennedy, this is really amazing work."

Amazing? Maggie The Wunderkin thought she'd done something amazing? Kennedy glanced out the window, searching the sky for flying pigs.

"Where did you learn to do all this?"

"On the job." Kennedy jerked a shoulder. "Over the years, I've worked in pretty much every segment of the hospitality industry, learning anything anybody would teach me."

Pru smiled at that. "You always were more of a hands-on learner."

"There's totally a market for this kind of thing," Athena agreed. "People who want to get the hell out of the city and have a more homey experience than a luxury hotel. Your sketches and business plan totally capture that. Good job, sis."

Praise. From Athena. Oh yeah, the devil was strapping on ice skates right about now.

"I ran the numbers myself, based on your projections," Maggie continued. "We could be open by Memorial Day."

Yep, she was definitely dreaming. "I'm sorry, it sounds like you actually want to *do* this."

"It's a totally viable plan with relatively minimal outlay to get started. The concept can be dialed up or down, depending on how the tourist sector develops in Eden's Ridge, and it would ultimately be self-sustaining, which is more than I can say for any of the ideas we came up with. Why wouldn't we want to do it?" Maggie asked.

"Because it's my idea. Because I'm the uneducated screw up, who's been off playing Peter Pan for a decade. Because you utterly lost your shit last night over what I'd already done."

"Did you really?" Athena asked, interested. "I've never seen you lose your shit."

Maggie scrubbed a hand over her face. "I'm sorry. You had no way of knowing, and I shouldn't have taken that out on you. Being back here stirs up all kinds of memories for me. But that's not really the point. Is that really what you think we—I—think of you?"

"You said, and I quote, that I've been 'drifting for a decade'. I've got no ambition, no training, no career, and you were worried I'd be more of a hindrance than a help."

"I—" Maggie closed her mouth. They all knew she couldn't deny it.

"I'm not sure any of us should be held accountable for the things we said right after Mom died," Pru put in.

"This is not new. It's not because Mom died. That just stripped off whatever filters we walk around with all the time. You've all been waiting for me to grow up since I left, and not a single one of you realized that I did. I grew up the moment I walked out that door. I had to because I was completely on my own, whether I was ready to be or not." Her hands fisted as all that remembered fear and absolute isolation came flooding back. The dam holding back all of it simply burst, the words coming in a torrent. "And I wasn't. I wasn't ready. I was so fucking scared, and I had no one." She was horrified to realize she was crying, but she was too damned tired to fight it back.

Suddenly she was in the middle of a tangle of arms as they all closed ranks around her.

"We had no idea." Pru's voice was choked with tears, too.

"We didn't know," Maggie said.

"I couldn't—" Kennedy choked on another sob.

"I know you couldn't tell us. I know." Maggie stroked her hair. "And it shouldn't have mattered. It should never have stopped us from seeing what you were going through. From taking more of an interest. I'm so damned sorry that our hurt got in the way of that. That we got caught up in all of my crap and didn't see any of yours. I never meant to make you feel like a screw up or an outsider. You've turned into an amazing, well-rounded woman, with a lot to offer, and I should never have made you feel like you couldn't contribute to the family."

"You're our sister, and we love you, no matter what. We should've made that clearer," Pru said.

"You're awesome," Ari put in. "Obviously."

Kennedy gave a watery laugh at that and buried her face in the teenager's hair.

"Helloooooooo. I'm still over here, and I have something to say." Athena's voice interrupted the group hug.

Kennedy sucked in a few breaths until she got herself under control. "I'm listening."

"I know I ragged on you pretty hard. Like everybody else, I had no idea why you left, and I was really angry with you for a long time. But I just want to say I'm sorry, and props to you for what you pulled off. I couldn't have done what you did. None of us could. So kudos. And thank you for having the vision for turning the house into an inn. Mom really would've loved that."

That almost set Kennedy off on a fresh bout of tears. The relief at finally being accepted by her family was sweeter than the honeysuckle just beginning to bloom outside. This was home, the family she'd been searching for through all her travels. This was love. "Thanks, y'all. I—well, I guess I've been carrying that around for a long time. It means a lot to know that you know and you get it. And that you like my idea."

"We love your idea," Pru said.

"I really look forward to working with you to finish fleshing out the details," Maggie added. "I think this has the potential to really be something great, not only for us, but for the Ridge."

Kennedy looked at her sisters and really felt connected to them for the first time in years. She took a deep breath as everything inside her began to settle. "I'd like that. But seriously, after some sleep."

"Oh! Of course. Go to bed," Pru ordered.

"And maybe when you get up, you could tell us about this book deal," Maggie put in.

Kennedy froze. "How did you...?"

"The proposal was mixed in with everything else."

Kennedy held still, feeling her soft underbelly exposed and waiting for more judgment.

"I was wrong. You did have direction and did have a career. It just wasn't what I expected them to look like. I'm really proud of you. And I'm sorry we made you feel like you couldn't tell us."

"It wasn't just that. In a lot of ways I saw myself the same way y'all did. It wasn't until I came home and had to start taking stock and justifying how I've spent my time that I started recognizing everything I've done and learned. So I can't really fault you for not having seen what I didn't see myself."

After another round of hugs and flurry of apologies, Kennedy finally climbed the stairs. Her feet felt leaden, but her heart was lighter than it had been for a decade. The curtains in her room were drawn, leaving the room bathed in shadow. She could just make out Xander sprawled in bed, breath slow and even. She undressed in the dark and slid beneath the covers beside him. His arms snaked out immediately to wrap around her and drag her back against him.

"Took so long?" he murmured.

"Just clearing the air with my sisters."

"Everything okay?"

She and her sisters probably had a long way to go to figure out this whole adult family thing, but this, Kennedy decided, was a really great start. She snuggled into Xander's embrace. "Everything's fine. Everything's really good. Go to back sleep, baby."

~

"WE'D LIKE to thank all of you for coming out today to this Memorial Day celebration of our grand opening."

Xander watched Kennedy where she stood on the front steps, flanked by all her sisters. A red ribbon stretched across the porch, from one rail to the other, and above them hung a sign, shrouded in fabric. The outside of the house looked much the same, with the azaleas in bloom and sunlight glinting off the freshly washed windows. But the inside had undergone a massive transformation over the past couple of months. He knew, as he'd helped with most of it. He was so proud to see how the sisters had come together in support of Kennedy's vision to make it a reality.

"This house has a long and fascinating history. For many of you here, it was a home for some length of time."

And indeed, the front lawn was covered in people, quite a few he remembered seeing at Joan's funeral. They sat on blankets or stood in clusters amid the scores of other locals who'd turned out for the open house and opening day picnic. Eden's Ridge had turned out en masse to check out its newest business.

"It's a house that's full of memories, a place where our mother still looms large, even though she's no longer with us. Joan Reynolds believed in making people at home, and we think she'd be proud to see how we intend to honor that going forward. For a variety of entirely practical reasons related to marketing and search engine optimization, we were going to call the place Reynolds House Bed and Breakfast. But in the end, we decided we'd rather defer to Mom because she named this house a long time ago."

Kennedy nodded and both Athena and Pru tugged on the strings they held. The fabric fell from the carved wooden sign announcing The Misfit Inn. A cheer went up from all the former fosters. Xander knew quite a few of them and their families had booked rooms over the course of the summer. After the pre-launch announcement Kennedy had made on her blog, the inn was already off to a solid start with bookings on into August.

The sisters crowded around an over-sized pair of scissors, lifting it to the ribbon. Cameras clicked. Grinning, one and all, they snipped it and shouted, "Welcome to The Misfit Inn!"

The crowd burst into applause and cheers. All four Reynolds sisters exchanged hugs. They'd made huge strides over the past weeks overcoming their misconceptions and working their way back to being a family. It had been good to see, good to know they were all finally healing.

Beside him, his mother laid a hand over her heart. "Oh, Joan would've loved this."

"Yeah, I think she would have."

Maggie lifted her voice above the din. "We invite you all to explore the house, see the guest rooms. There's food in the kitchen. Please, come in and enjoy yourselves!"

Xander was at the head of the pack, snagging Kennedy around the waist and dragging her into one of the side rooms.

"What are you doing? We have visitors."

"They can wait." He swung her around, lacing his hands at the small of her back and beaming. "I'm so damned proud of you. You did this. You brought this place into being."

"Not without a lot of help."

"Your vision," he insisted. "And now it's a reality."

She pressed her lips to his in a lightning kiss. "Thank you. But the reality is that we have most of town here, and I need to play hostess."

"Kennedy this is—oh! I'm so sorry."

Xander pivoted to see a tall brunette in the doorway.

"Elena! You made it!" Kennedy broke away to fling her arms around the other woman.

"Wouldn't have missed it. This is an amazing turnout."

"We're pretty pumped." She held out her hand to him. "Xander, this is Elena Beckhoff. My editor."

Xander grinned. So this was the woman making Kennedy's book a reality. "Pleased to meet you."

Elena shook his hand, giving him a once over from head to toe before looking back to Kennedy. "You ever considered writing romance? Because, girl, you've got some excellent book fodder right here."

Kennedy beamed at him. "I really do.

If only she knew.

"Xander's the sheriff here in Stone County."

"Interim," he corrected. He'd stepped into the role right after his father's heart attack.

"Just until the election." Buck stepped into the room, a plate of appetizers in his hand. "Everybody knows you're the right man for the job."

He was almost back to himself, a fact which greatly relieved Xander. He didn't ever want to see that gray cast to his father's face again. This was the first major event in town since his doctor had cleared him to go back to normal life. Since Buck was officially retired now, he was still figuring out what that looked like, but he was throwing himself into campaigning on Xander's behalf. It was an olive branch Xander had opted to take, both because he despised campaigning himself and because he'd realized Kennedy was right. Forgiveness wasn't for his father. It was for him.

"Dad, you're not supposed to be eating bacon. Your doctor said."

"No, it's fine. I had Athena make a special stack for him with turkey bacon so he could be included," Kennedy said. "Although...that doesn't look like turkey bacon."

"It's not." Athena charged into the room and plucked the plate right out of Buck's hand and gave him another. "*These* are yours."

His father eyed the bacon wrapped pears on his plate. "Turkey bacon? That's a crime against food."

"On that we agree, old man."

Kennedy plucked one of the pears off the confiscated plate and bit in. "Mmm, this is good. What is that? Cinnamon?"

"And a pinch of ginger. It'll be a super simple appetizer you can make once I head back to Chicago. I've been working on some menus."

"Sounds awesome." Kennedy turned and made a presenting gesture with one hand. "Elena, this is my sister the Michelin-starred chef, Athena. Athena, my editor."

Elena shook Athena's hand and tried one of the pears herself. "This is amazing."

"You should try the rest of the spread."

"Don't mind if I do." The two women headed for the kitchen. "Have you ever considered writing a cookbook? It's not my area, but I've got a colleague..."

His father trailed after them, probably intent on finding something more interesting than turkey bacon.

Okay, Xander was going to have to wait at least a little while before enacting his plan. He kissed Kennedy again, then nudged her along. "Go, do your thing. I'll catch up with you later."

As Kennedy mingled, Xander wandered through himself, visiting with people, talking about the renovations. The tone was one of celebration. He wondered if the girls felt the difference from the last time the house was full of people.

"Xander, have you met Robert Barth?" Maggie gestured to an older guy with a receding hairline that he remembered seeing at the funeral.

"The attorney, right?"

"That'd be me. Nice to see you again, Sheriff."

When was Xander going to get used to that?

"Robert has been helping us sort out Mom's estate and what our options are with Ari."

"Yeah?" They'd all been so busy with prepping the inn the last couple of months, he wasn't sure where things stood with their youngest family member.

Ari herself popped up. "Apparently they get to go from being my sisters to my moms."

"Looks like the next step will be formal certification as foster parents." Maggie explained.

"There's no question that Ari is better off staying here, so it shouldn't be too difficult a process," Robert said.

Xander draped an arm around the girl's shoulders. "What do you think about that, squirt?"

She shrugged. "It'll be a little weird I guess. But whatever. I get to stay."

"That you do." Maggie smiled.

Ari poked him in the ribs and whispered sotto voce, "Did you talk to Kennedy yet?"

"Not yet." Xander made a throat slashing motion.

The girl hip checked him. "Well, hurry up. She's in the office with Pru."

"Yeah, yeah. I'm getting there." Xander estimated that enough time had passed that the guests were mostly fed and had been greeted. He probably could manage to steal Kennedy away for a bit.

She and Pru were bent over the computer.

"We just got a reservation for *a month*," Pru exclaimed. "One Flynn Bohannon, at the end of June."

"Flynn!" Kennedy clapped her hands with glee. "He's a good friend of mine from Ireland. An exceptionally talented musician. You're gonna love him. Oh, it'll be so good to see him."

"I look forward to meeting him." Xander grabbed her hand. "Pru, can I borrow Kennedy for a bit?"

Pru waved them off. "Go, go. Everything's under control here."

"Great." He pulled Kennedy through the house, snaking through the crowd and out the back door.

Laughing, she hurried to keep up. "Where are we going?"

"For a little walk."

"Now?"

"Yep, now." Because he couldn't wait anymore to get her away from all the people.

He headed down the trail toward their spot, only slowing once the sounds of revelry faded.

"Feeling a little claustrophobic?" she asked.

"Little bit. I just wanted some one-on-one time with you."

"Couldn't wait until tonight?" Her lips curved into a teasing smile.

"Not why I pulled you away, but I'll never say no to that." A mental image of making love to her outside, in the daylight, her golden hair tumbled, those green eyes full of passion and secrets had him going hard.

"Well, they probably won't miss me for half an hour or so."

"Temptress. Maybe later."

The trail began to rise and the trees began to thin, opening up to a wide vista of mountain, covered in gorgeous swaths of color. Purples and whites and happy golds highlighted rich, verdant slopes. Pulling her to a stop at the edge of their overlook, he wrapped his arms around her and took in the view.

Sighing, she relaxed back against him. "It's beautiful here. Of all the places I went, all the sights I saw, nowhere was ever quite like this."

Heart drumming, Xander pressed a kiss to the shoulder bared by her sundress. "Do you know why I nicknamed you Lark all those years ago?"

She tipped her head back to look at him, curiosity flickering over her face. "I assumed because I was spontaneous and always game to go on one. Or maybe because of the singing."

He smiled. "There's that, but no. It was because of this." Xander bent to pluck one of the deep purple flowers. "This is purple larkspur."

Her nose wrinkled in a way that made him want to kiss it. "You nicknamed me after a flower? That seems like something more suited to Pru."

"It's a wildflower that grows here in the Smokies. Wildflowers are pretty amazing things, actually. They look all soft and delicate, but they're actually surprisingly tough. They grow and bloom where they're planted, no matter the conditions. You've done that all your life, wherever you landed. And I picked this one because it symbolizes an open heart, because it grows here, where you gave me yours."

He'd stunned her. Kennedy's pretty, painted mouth opened and closed a little like a fish, her eyes taking on a bit of a sheen.

"Xander."

Reaching out, he stroked her cheek, tucking a lock of hair behind her ear. "I never expected to get it back. Never expected to stand here with you again, and I can't tell you how grateful I am to be wrong."

"You're going to make me cry."

His lips curved. "Hold off on that a minute. I'm not done."

"I had no idea there was going to be a speech."

"Not a speech. Just a question." Skimming a hand down her arm, Xander laced his fingers with hers and brought them to his lips. "I love you—more than anything—and I want to know, Kennedy Elaine Reynolds, if you'll stay here with me and put down the forever kind of roots." He pulled the ring from his pocket and sank to one knee. "Will you marry me?"

Kennedy gave a hiccupping sort of noise, somewhere between

a sob and a laugh, and dropped to her knees, throwing her arms around his shoulders and raining kisses over his face.

Laughing, he did the same. "Can I take that as a yes?"

"Yes! Yes. Yes. A thousand times, yes."

He captured her hand and slid the ring on, watching the diamond wink in the May sunshine.

Tipping her head to his, she gave a happy sigh. "How do you feel about a June wedding?"

"Beautiful time of year up here," he said. He didn't care when they got married, so long as she was his in the end.

"It's not a lot of time, but I'll put Maggie on it. She can plan anything fast."

"Wait, like *next month?*"

Kennedy pulled back. "Too soon?"

Grinning, Xander reeled her back in. "No such thing." And amid the larkspur and columbine and mountain laurel, he kissed his future wife.

THOSE SWEET WORDS

THE MISFIT INN #2

Good old, reliable Pru. Of the four Reynolds sisters, Pru is the natural choice to take on custody of the girl their late mother had planned to adopt. At thirty, suddenly becoming the mom of a teenager means big changes, but Pru's ready to do whatever it takes to adopt Ari. Before she settles down, though, she wants one thing for herself.

Enter Flynn Bohannon, the sinfully sexy Irish musician in town for her sister's wedding. He's led the kind of free, vagabond life Pru can hardly imagine. Definitely not the kind of guy she should be dating, but he's the perfect guy for a crazy fun fling before her life changes. When Pru proposes a brief, no strings affair, Flynn's not about to say no. But when unexpected complications endanger the adoption, the two find themselves in a phony engagement.

Now they have to convince a sharp-eyed, skeptical social worker, a teen who's too smart for her own good, three dubious sisters, and one protective brother-in-law that

Flynn's willing to give up the gypsy life and settle down. But in convincing everyone that this relationship is real, will they convince each other as well?

Chapter One

"There is no way I'm moving into your newlywed love shack."

Pru Reynolds froze, holding in a wince as the object of the current discussion made herself known. Of *course* Ari had been skulking outside the kitchen. How many times had Pru herself done the same as a child? There never seemed to be another option when the grown-ups were deciding your fate without consulting you. She'd hated it. Hated being at the mercy of a bunch of relative strangers—even well-intentioned ones. But that's what it was to be part of the foster system. That was the fate that Pru and her sister, Kennedy, were trying to save Ari from.

Pru turned to face the girl, taking in the dark, stormy eyes and the mulish set to her mouth. "Nothing's been decided, sugar. We aren't going to make that decision for you." It was important to get that out there. To make Ari understand that she had a choice here. Foster kids had so few actual choices, and fighting that sense of powerlessness was one of the biggest hurdles to overcome.

"Yeah," Kennedy added. "We were just reviewing your options, discussing the pros and cons, so we could present them in a nice, organized fashion."

Ari arched one eyebrow in a move that displayed all of her barely teenaged disdain. Not yet fourteen, she was going to be a pistol, as their mother used to say.

Pru rode out the instant lash of pain at the thought of Joan. It had been just under four months since they'd lost her to a car accident. Just under four months since she and her three sisters had taken charge of the girl Joan had been in the process of adopting. Joan had meant Ari to be one of them—the last and youngest Reynolds sister. But the legalities hadn't been finished, so Pru and Kennedy, and Kennedy's fiancé, Xander, had all undergone the necessary certification classes to serve as her foster parents. Not something Pru had expected to be doing at thirty—prospectively taking on a teenaged daughter. But she'd be damned if she'd let the girl go back into the system. Ari was family.

"Come on and sit down. We'll talk about this," Pru told her.

Ari crossed her arms, but she came over and plopped down at the big farmhouse table.

"Do you want tea?" Pru asked.

One shoulder lifted in a shrug. "Sure."

Pru moved to the stove and reminded herself that the attitude was better than the complete, withdrawn silence after Joan's death.

"So, here's the deal, kiddo," Kennedy began. "The great state of Tennessee has officially declared Pru, me, and Xander fit as foster parents. Well, we've passed all the classes, anyway."

Pru pulled mugs from the cabinet and began to fill tea balls with the loose leaf black tea she favored. "The next step is the home study, so we have to let Mae know whether she'll be doing that on me or on Kennedy and Xander. All of us are more than willing, so it's your choice."

Their situation was highly unusual. Officially, they shouldn't have had Ari at all until all the certifications had been passed and the home study completed. But their mother had been a foster parent for more than twenty-five years and a social worker before that. Mae Bradley, Ari's case worker, had known Joan all that time, and on Joan's death, she'd pulled some strings with the powers that be, convincing them that it was in the best interest of the child to stay put with someone familiar. God bless small towns.

"You're getting married this weekend and going off on your honeymoon to Timbuktu—" Ari said.

"The UK," Kennedy corrected, smiling a little as Pru set a mug of tea in front of her.

"—and I'm not gonna be moving in when you get back and stepping all over your newlywed toes. I *like* you and Xander. Why would I do that to you? Congratulations, Mr. and Mrs. Kincaid. Welcome home! And oh, by the way, here's your teenager! That'd put an end to the honeymoon right quick."

Kennedy reached out to cover the girl's hand with her own. "Ari, Xander and I love you. It wouldn't be like that."

Ari pulled away, wrapping her hands around the mug Pru gave her. "You and Xander lost ten years. You deserve some time to be just together."

Pru couldn't argue with the truth of that. But it was Kennedy who'd first managed to pull Ari out of her shell after the funeral, so maybe she was the best sister for the job. Pru didn't care to analyze the pang she felt at that thought. "The home study will take some time. I expect, if you wanted it, Mae would be happy to do home studies on all of us. Then, you could stay with me, while the lovebirds have their time, and go to them when you felt like you were ready."

Ari was already shaking her head. "I want to stay here, with you. I want to keep my room and help with the inn." She dropped her gaze to her mug, jiggling the tea ball. When she spoke again, her voice was small. "You were there from the beginning, and I want to be a Reynolds, not a Kincaid."

Pru's throat went thick. She exchanged a glance with Kennedy, who nodded slightly. "Then that's what we'll do."

Ari looked up and the guarded hope on her face cut Pru to the bone. "Really? You'll really adopt me, like Joan was going to?"

It wasn't a decision she made lightly. She knew what it meant to be wanted, to have the stability of a good forever home. Joan had done that for her, for her sisters, and provided a safe place to land for countless others, over the years. Pru might not have any intention of stepping fully into her mother's shoes, but for this one child, she'd do whatever it took.

"If that's what you want, then yeah. I'd like that. I'd like that very much."

Ari grinned, her temper fading with the speed of a summer storm. "Then I guess I'll have to start working on calling you Mom."

The word hit Pru in the chest like a sucker punch. Mom. She was going to be a mom. This was going to be her daughter. She was going to be fully responsible for another person's...everything. Holy crap.

"It'll take us both some getting used to," she managed.

Ari slid off the bench and came around the table to give Pru a quick hug. She wasn't touch shy like so many kids Pru had known, so Pru gave her a hearty squeeze, as her own mother would have done. Over the girl's thin shoulder, she saw Kennedy beaming.

"Just to try out my mom voice, have you done your sweep of the guest rooms to see if any of the TP or linens or complimentary toiletries need restocking before the next guests arrive?"

"Not yet."

"Hop to. The Johnsons are supposed to be here by six-thirty."

Ari saluted and scurried off.

"Congratulations, Mom. And you even did it without the baby weight," Kennedy teased.

Pru sagged back in her chair. "Jesus."

Her sister sobered. "Are you really okay with this?"

"Yes. I wouldn't have told her I'd do it, if I wasn't. I'm just...a little overwhelmed." And a little bit jealous that she'd be doing this alone.

Oh, Kennedy and Xander would help out. So would her

other sisters, Athena and Maggie, whenever they were in town. But there'd be no husband helping her share the load or the joys. She envied Kennedy that. She'd assumed she'd meet someone eventually, but Eden's Ridge was a tiny town, with a shallow dating pool. Unlike her sisters, she hadn't left, other than to finish her training as a massage therapist. Eden's Ridge was home. She'd found no grand passion here, and up until they'd begun planning Kennedy's whirlwind wedding, Pru had been fine with that.

She'd be fine with it again. Her mother had led a full and rich life without partner. She could do the same. If she felt a twinge of self-pity at that, she shoved it away. Ari was the priority. Taking care of her was what Joan would have wanted.

"It's a big step," Kennedy said. "I'd be worried if you didn't feel a little overwhelmed."

"That's probably been a little exacerbated by the fact that we've planned your wedding in a month. Thank God for Cayla Black." A friend from high school, Cayla was divorced and back in the Ridge with her four-year-old daughter, trying to get an event planning business off the ground. She'd jumped at the chance to use Kennedy as a guinea pig.

"She is, indeed, awesome," Kennedy concurred. "I don't even think Maggie could've done better."

"It helps that you don't care too much about the details beyond being married to Xander in the end."

"True enough. Speaking of, I want to swing by the house to see my other half before I head into work for the night." She rose and came around to hug Pru herself. "Mom would love that you're doing this for Ari."

"I know. And it helps a little bit. She feels kind of like a last piece of Mom."

"Are you gonna call Maggie and Athena to tell them the news?"

"They'll be here in two days for wedding festivities. I'll tell them in person. Go forth and squeeze in whatever canoodling you can manage."

Kennedy rolled her eyes. "Canoodling. You sound like Ari."

"Fitting since she's going to be mine." Pru felt another flutter in her belly. That would stop being scary at some point, right?

"Touché. Love you, Pru."

"Love you back."

When she was gone, Pru took their tea—now cold—and dumped it out. She popped her own into the microwave, then carried the mug back to her room. Formerly her mother's room. She'd moved in formally after she and her sisters had converted the old Victorian into a bed and breakfast to save the family estate. It was a long way from profitable yet, but they'd had steady bookings since they opened Memorial Day weekend and plenty more that stretched out well into the fall.

Sinking down into the overstuffed chair, she tugged open the drawer and pulled out the photo album with "My Kids" embossed across the front. She'd found it in the course of cleaning out. This book contained photos of every single child her mother had fostered over the years. There were so many.

Had her mother felt this bone deep panic at the beginning? Wondering whether she could do this? Whether she'd irrevocably mess these kids up? Or had she always been the unflappable, down-to-earth woman Pru remembered? With the weight of the decision she'd just made pressing down, she needed her mother's comfort. So, tea in hand, she opened the cover and slid into memory.

∼

"What's the status update on the wedding?"

"For God's sake, Maggie, we've been here all of five minutes. Can't you wait to try to run things until we've had some time to breathe?" Athena complained.

Maggie shot her a cool look. "The wedding is in five days. There's no time to relax."

And my sisters are officially home, Pru thought.

"We hired a wedding planner. And Pru's here. Shit's being handled. Right?" Athena looked to Pru for confirmation.

Her lips twitched. "Shit is, indeed, being handled." That her sisters trusted her to do exactly that was both flattering and maddening.

"See there? Now relax, woman." Athena flopped down on the overstuffed sofa.

"Might I remind you that there are little ears present, so perhaps tone things down from the language you use in your restaurant kitchen?" Pru suggested.

Ari and Athena both rolled their eyes.

"Gordon Ramsey is worse," Ari said. When Pru arched a brow, she just shrugged. "What? I really like *Kitchen Nightmares*."

There was no need to ask who got her hooked on that.

"Oh, did you see that episode with that poser in Ohio?" Athena asked.

"'I can cook, Joe,'" Ari said, in a passable parody of the celebrity chef.

"That was *brutal*," Athena agreed.

"Well deserved," Ari pronounced.

Deciding she was just grateful the two were bonding, Pru turned her attention to Maggie. "To answer your question, everything is going fine. Our bridesmaid dresses are ready and waiting. You and Athena have your final fitting tomorrow. The photographer is lined up, and Mrs. Lowrey, from church, is making the cake."

"You're not doing the cake?" Ari asked Athena.

"I'm a chef, not a baker. I *can* bake. I choose not to."

"Plus, Mrs. Lowrey makes the *best* red velvet cake in the state," Kennedy announced, sailing into the room with a tray of drinks from the kitchen. "She has a blue ribbon from the state fair that says so."

"What about music?" Maggie asked.

"My friend, Flynn, will be playing."

"Oh, did you finally talk to him about it?" Pru had heard plenty about the Irish musician Kennedy had toured with for a while, during her time abroad. He'd been one of the first to book a room after they opened the inn.

"No. He's playing his way down the East coast. Not quite sure where he is just now, and his cell phone doesn't work in the States. But he'll be here in a couple of days. It's not like he's going to say no. It's my *wedding*."

Maggie pinched the bridge of her nose and moved her mouth in something that might have been a silent prayer or a curse. "Okay, so what's left?"

"Just decorating the barn for the ceremony and getting tables set up for the reception. And we'll have help with that. Everybody who's got a room booked from tomorrow through the weekend is one of Mom's former fosters. And there are more coming in day of," Pru told her.

Maggie's shoulders relaxed a little. Kennedy swung an arm around them. "Did you think you were going to have to wade in and sort out chaos?"

"It wouldn't be the first time. But I should have known better. I can always rely on Pru to have my back." She flashed a grateful smile.

Pru just shrugged. "It's what I do."

"Is there anything else I need to know about?"

From the sofa, Ari began to bounce.

"You got ants in your pants, kid?" Athena asked.

Ari looked at Pru, and it was impossible to hold back the smile.

"She's excited because she's finally going to be a Reynolds. I'm adopting her."

"Whoa." Athena hooked Ari around the neck and pulled her into a headlock. "Welcome to the family, kid."

Maggie smiled at the giggling teen, who was digging her fingers into Athena's sides in a vain effort to tickle her. "That's wonderful."

"There are still some steps to go through, but that's the plan," Pru said.

The doorbell rang.

"Are we expecting more guests?" Kennedy asked. "I didn't think we had anybody else booked for tonight."

"Not guests. Your surprise," Pru said. "Ari, you want to go get the door?"

"'Kay!" Red-faced and gasping, she rolled off the sofa and raced out of the room. Moments later, she came back, a smiling blonde in tow.

"Hail, hail, the gang's all here," the blonde called. "Welcome home, y'all."

"Abbey Whittaker! I had no idea you were back in the Ridge." Maggie crossed the room to give her a hug.

"Only been back a couple of weeks. Grandaddy Whittaker isn't doing so great. His dementia is getting worse, so I came back to help out, while the family figures out what to do about it."

"I'm so sorry to hear that. But I'm definitely glad to see you. Weren't you off in Atlanta?"

"That's where I headed when Pru and I finished school, but I wound up moving to Mississippi last year. I've got kin in Wishful—Granddaddy's brother and his branch of the family are there. I've been working at a swank spa in Wishful."

"Which is why she's here tonight," Pru said. "She's giving all of us spa treatments."

"All natural and guaranteed to rejuvenate and relax."

Athena jerked a thumb at Maggie. "This one definitely needs to relax."

Abbey laughed. "And what about the bride to be?"

"Pretty sure she's the most laid back one here," Pru said.

"She's in luuuuuurve," Ari sang.

"It shows. Hard to duplicate that kind of glow with even the best products. You look great."

Kennedy beamed. "Thanks. Being happy agrees with me."

"The regular nookie doesn't hurt," Athena added.

Pru clapped her hands over Ari's ears. "Athena!"

"What? It's true."

Ari tugged the hands away. "Joan already had the talk with me. Great sex between mature, committed individuals is good for your mental health."

Pru's mouth fell open, but nothing came out. Her face felt frozen somewhere between horror and laughter.

"Well, she's not wrong," Kennedy admitted.

Maybe that's what's wrong with me. No great sex in.... Have I ever had truly great sex? When was the last time I had even mediocre sex? Oh, dear God, why am I thinking about this now?

Cheeks burning, Pru looked at Abbey, who was valiantly trying not to snicker. "Our mom was really big on female empowerment. But for you, young lady, that can wait until you're twenty-five." She grabbed Ari by the shoulders and marched her toward the kitchen, laughter in their wake as everyone trailed behind.

Abbey unloaded the bags she'd brought and began mixing ingredients, while Kennedy rounded up a bunch of towels. As she created multiple bowls of fragrant glop, Abbey scanned them all. "So, other than the bride, who else is tripping down the relationship highway? Or dating? Or anything involving the prospect of a significant other? Because I most definitely am not, and I need to live vicariously through somebody."

"Those Mississippi boys not doing it for you?" Athena asked.

"There's one very serious problem with them—it seems all the good ones are taken."

"It's a definite problem in small towns," Pru agreed. "I can't remember the last time I had a date."

"Didn't you go out with Gavin Harkness around Christmas?" Maggie asked.

"I went to dinner with him. For what I *thought* was just a meal between joint committee members for that Angel Tree fundraiser. I didn't realize he thought it was a date until he tried to kiss me when he brought me home. I turned my face at the last second and he hit my cheek. Then he just kind of froze there for several seconds, until I managed to twist the doorknob and escape. It was…awkward."

"Well, it's not like the city is any better for prospects," Maggie said. "In L.A., everybody meets people with an eye for how they can be used to further their career. There's no such thing as a simple girl meets guy on an elevator and gets asked to dinner, for a night of conversation about mutual interests. Instead, he's asking enough questions during the salad course, you feel like you're in the middle of a job interview."

Abbey grimaced. "That sounds awful. Please tell me you skipped dessert."

"I gave serious thought to disappearing to the bathroom and never coming back. But he knew my boss, as it turns out, so I stuck it out."

"What about you, Athena?" Abbey asked.

"I intimidate men."

"Shocker," Kennedy murmured.

The impact of the middle finger Athena shot up was somewhat mitigated by the bright green avocado mask smeared all over her face.

"So, other than the bride, we're all failing in the dating department. Y'all, this is a sad state of affairs. We are smart, sexy, available women. What is wrong with all these men?" Abbey came back to the table, passing out warm, wet wash cloths. "Everybody wipe off your mask with firm, downward strokes from the center line of your face."

Kennedy rubbed at the bentonite clay mask already flaking off her face. "Maybe I should hook y'all up with some of Xander's single friends. All of his groomsmen are available."

"Please," Athena snorted. "Porter was one of our brothers."

"That still leaves Logan and Jonah," Kennedy pointed out.

"Athena and I don't live here, so that seems a pointless effort. But maybe one of them would suit Pru." Maggie angled her head, studying Pru from across the table.

"Hello, I'm sitting right here and *not* looking for a setup, thanks very much. I do not need a pity date. I haven't even thought about dating—" She cut herself off before *since Mom died* could spill out. No reason to drag the group down. "Besides, I've got enough on my plate with the inn and the fact that I'm acquiring a teenager."

"Yeah, but at least I came housebroken," Ari said.

"Girl's got a point. Men are so much harder to train than dogs," Athena agreed. She patted her face dry. "Dude, my skin feels amazing."

"Mine's all tingly," Maggie said.

Abbey set a small bowl on the table. "Here, each of you slather some of this on. It's specially made moisturizer. No chemicals."

"It feels wonderful. All of it does," Pru said. "You know, a lot of my massage clients would love this. What would you think about doing some freelance spa treatments, while you're here? We could set up some space for you to work out of."

"That would be wonderful. The Babylon is holding my job, but it would be great to keep my hand in things. Plus, I'll need a break from Granddaddy."

"Great. We'll set a time after the wedding to discuss terms."

"Sounds like a plan." Abbey removed the double boiler she'd had simmering at the stove. "Now, who wants a paraffin bath for your hands?"

Flynn Bohannon lived a gypsy's life, traveling from town to town, venue to venue, sharing the music of his homeland. To his way of thinking, there was nothing better than seeing new faces, new places, every few days. If things began to feel a little stale, he picked up stakes and found somewhere new. Sometimes he traveled in a group, jamming with other musicians he met along the way. Other times, like now, he was a solo act. Either worked fine for him. It was all about the music.

He'd landed in Boston three weeks before and had been working his way down the Eastern seaboard, playing in pubs, bars, taverns, and coffee shops—a different town or city every night. Some shows had been pre-booked. Others, like the pick-up session he'd had in that pub in Baltimore, where the bartender had turned out to be the cousin of a friend of his mother's, had been a delightful, impulsive surprise. Flynn liked surprises. Which was why he'd made his way to Eden's Ridge, Tennessee a day early.

He'd wanted to surprise one of his dearest friends. And, he admitted, he hoped to catch her before she'd put on her *everything's fine* face and get a real read on how she was doing. Kennedy Reynolds had been every bit the gypsy he was, and now she'd come home and decided to settle here out of family obligation. Not that he frowned on that. There was a child involved. But he wondered how long it would take her to feel choked by the roots she'd long ago escaped.

It was beautiful. He'd give her that. These were younger, wilder mountains than he was used to. There simply weren't this many trees in the mountains of Ireland. At home, the peaks had been whittled down by wind and weather and time, until they'd been reduced to their bare essentials. Wild, yes, but often barren but for the grasses and scrub. Here the trees stretched in a lush, green blanket as far as the eye could see. As he navigated the switchbacks, he noted the craggy rocks peeking through here and there, but otherwise, everything was alive with the vibrant colors of summer.

The house was set back in the trees, a charming Victorian painted a mystical greenish gray, with crisp, white trim. He'd have recognized it from Kennedy's description, even without the wooden sign above the porch proclaiming The Misfit Inn. It rose a towering three stories high, with a turret to one side. The porch wrapped all the way round, with fanciful scrollwork at the corners and various groupings of chairs or gliders set to take in the view, which was magnificent from nearly all angles. There was the old bodock tree Kennedy had used to sneak in and out of the house as a girl. And beyond it, the barn, doors thrown wide.

Flynn found a place to park and climbed out. He knocked on the big front door, and when no one answered, he circled around back, scanning for Kennedy's familiar blonde head. He followed sounds of music—a cheerful country tune about some lass calling dibs—into the barn. The space inside was clear. White drapes had been hung above to block off what he presumed was a hay loft. Dozens of folding chairs were stacked to one side. And in the center of the barn, at the top of a ladder, a woman stretched to wrap white twinkle lights around a barn rafter. As he stood, undetected, she joined in the chorus with cheerful alto.

Charmed, he stayed where he was, watching. She was all soft curves, a fact made evident by the stretch of shorts across her perfect, lush backside. Flynn took a moment of reverence for that magnificent ass, captivated by the gentle flex of it as she worked and twitched her hips to the rhythm on the radio. *Now that is a woman.* He'd know, as he'd made quite the study of them the world over.

The ass ended in tanned legs and sport sandals. Stifling an appreciative murmur, Flynn lifted his gaze higher, noting the swatch of olive skin between the waistband of her shorts and the t-shirt riding high as she reached to continue the wrap. He realized then that she was far too short to be doing this. She'd gone above that last safety step of the ladder trying to reach the beam well above her head. Even as he thought to speak up, the ladder began to wobble. The woman sucked in a breath, flailing for any kind of purchase.

Flynn leapt forward as the ladder toppled and the woman screamed. He didn't exactly catch her so much as break her fall, but he managed to wrap his arms around her as she crashed down, softening the impact as they both hit the ground. They both lay there, stunned, wrapped in a tangle. As she lifted her head and trained those wide, dark eyes on his, Flynn couldn't help but think his breathlessness and pounding heart weren't entirely from the collision.

I'm callin' dibs, indeed.

He couldn't stop himself from reaching out to brush the hair back from that exquisite face. "Are you all right, then?"

"Flynn?"

Well, and wasn't it a fine thing to hear his name on those lips, in that soft Southern twang? As if she'd been waiting just for him, for this moment. The sound of it did something to him, plucking some chord deep in his soul until it sang. Could she feel it where her hands pressed against his chest?

"You're early," she said.

"Seems to me, I'm right on time."

Her pupils sprang wide at that, and she sucked in a breath. His gaze dropped to those lips, and his hand tightened at the curve of her waist. Only the sound of running footsteps kept him from leaning in to taste her.

"I heard a crash. What—Oh my God, Pru, are you okay?"

Pru. Which made her Kennedy's eldest sister.

Christ. He needed to get ahold of himself. Flynn relaxed his grip and leaned back. Seeming to collect herself, Pru shifted from his lap—more was the pity—and reached up to take the offered hand. That was when he realized the owner of the hand was a young girl.

"I'm fine. The ladder tipped."

The girl, who had to be Ari, looked down at him with bright, curious eyes. "Who'd you land on?"

Flynn rolled to his feet, offering his hand, as more people came into the barn, including the familiar face he'd come looking for.

"Flynn Bohannon!"

He grinned and opened his arms wide. When Kennedy leapt into them, he swung her in a circle. "It's good to see you, *deifiúr beag*."

"Back atcha, boy-o! We weren't expecting you until tomorrow."

"I thought I'd surprise you. But I seem to have interrupted some sort of festivities. Are you getting ready for a party, then?"

"Oh, yeah, about that. There's someone I want you to meet." Kennedy pulled back and held her hand out to a broad-shouldered man, with close-cropped brown hair and a steady gaze. He slid his arm around her shoulders, and she looked up at him with absolute adoration. "Xander, this is my brother from another mother, Flynn. Flynn, Xander Kincaid, my fiancé."

Flynn's mouth fell open. "Your what now?"

Kennedy laughed. "It's our wedding we're decorating for. We're getting married on Saturday."

"Married?" Flynn repeated. Was she insane? She'd been home, what, four months? If that.

She laughed again, fairly glowing with happiness. "It's a long story, and I'll tell you all about it over a pint later. First, I want you to meet my family. This is Ari." She laid her hands on the shoulders of the young Hispanic girl, with the dark, soulful eyes and ready grin.

"Pleased to meet you," Flynn said, shaking her hand.

"And this is Pru."

"We've met," they said in unison.

Kennedy arched her brows.

"She fell out of the sky," Flynn said.

"More properly, I fell off a ladder," Pru corrected. "Thanks for saving me from breaking my neck."

He mimed doffing a hat and bowed. "Happy to be of service, milady. Perhaps you'll let someone taller assist you in finishing with the lights?"

Pru flushed. "Oh, you're a guest. I'm not—oh my God, your room's not ready." She looked, if possible, even more flustered by that than she had crashing into him.

She was already turning toward the door, when Flynn caught her hand. "It's fine. Don't trouble on my account. I arrived early and unannounced. Just shove me in a closet or something. I'll be fine." That sent his mind off on a merry little jaunt, imagining what it would be like to drag Pru into a linen closet and get to know the rest of those lovely curves.

She looked scandalized, and he wondered if he'd said that aloud. Or maybe it was that he'd been rubbing circles on the back of her hand with his thumb.

"You're a guest at our inn. You'll have a proper room. Just give me fifteen minutes—twenty at the outside."

"Psh," Kennedy snorted. "He's family."

"The family all have beds," Pru argued.

Now was definitely *not* the time to suggest sharing hers. And really, he needed to quash this whole reaction. This was Kennedy's *sister*.

"Fine. You fix a room. *I'm* putting him to work. He and Xander can finish with the lights. Maggie and Athena should be back from their fitting soon, and it's Athena's turn to cook dinner."

Pru tugged her hand free and started for the door. "Fifteen minutes," she repeated. "Ari, come help me please."

Because he wanted to watch her go, Flynn deliberately turned toward the ladder and righted it. "Right. Lights?"

"To start." Kennedy grinned.

He propped an arm on one of the rungs and gave her the side eye. "Oh, so that's how it is? You're going to make me work for my supper?"

"I'm going to make you play for it. I want you to play for the wedding. Will you? I know it's last minute and all, but you're here and there's no one else I'd rather hear."

Flynn still wanted to know the story behind this sudden rush to the altar. But given her fiancé was watching him from ten feet away, he opted for the only safe answer. "I'd be honored."

Kennedy threw her arms around him in another, staggering hug. "Oh, thank you!"

"Anything for you. Now, where are the rest of these lights?"

Get your copy today!

ABOUT KAIT

Kait is a Mississippi native, who often swears like a sailor, calls everyone sugar, honey, or darlin', and can wield a bless your heart like a saber or a Snuggie, depending on requirements.

You can find more information on Kait and her books on her website http://kaitnolan.com. While you're there, sign up for her newsletter so you don't miss out on news about new releases!

OTHER BOOKS BY KAIT NOLAN

A full and up-to-date list of Kait's books can be found at http://kaitnolan.com

The Misfit Inn Series
When You Got A Good Thing (Kennedy and Xander)
Once Upon A Wedding (Misty and Denver)
Those Sweet Words (Pru and Flynn)

Wishful Series
Once Upon A Coffee (Avery and Dillon) **Included in *Wish I Might***
To Get Me To You (Cam and Norah)
Be Careful, It's My Heart (Brody and Tyler)
Know Me Well (Liam and Riley)
Once Upon A Setup (A Meet Cute Romance with Piper and Myles!) **Included in *Be Careful, It's My Heart*.**
Just For This Moment (Myles and Piper)
Wish I Might (Reed and Cecily)
Turn My World Around (Tucker and Corinne)
Dance Me A Dream (Jace and Tara)
See You Again (Trey and Sandy)
The Christmas Fountain (Chad and Mary Alice)

Wishing For a Hero Series (A Wishful Spinoff Series)
If I Didn't Care (Judd and Autumn)

~

Meet Cute Romance
Once Upon A Snow Day (**Included in** *Dance Me A Dream*)
Once Upon A New Year's Eve (Included in *The Christmas Fountain*)
Once Upon An Heirloom (**Included in** *See You Again*)
Once Upon A Coffee (**Included in** *Wish I Might*)
Once Upon A Setup (**Included in** *Be Careful, It's My Heart*)
Once Upon A Campfire (**Included in** *Second Chance Summer*)
Once Upon A Wedding

Printed in Great Britain
by Amazon